Praise for Pamela Carter Joern's novel *Floor of the Sky*

Winner of the Nebraska Book Award, sponsored by the Nebraska
  Center for the Book
Winner of the Alex Award, sponsored by the Young Adult
  Library Services Association
Barnes & Noble Discover Great New Writers selection

"Playwright Joern's characters are as stern as the land, and the
world of her debut novel is sturdy and memorable."
      —*Publishers Weekly*

"Joern intricately weaves together a compelling family saga and
a beautifully rendered paean to the land her characters love and
are struggling to preserve. . . . Joern's lyrical and painterly descrip-
tions of the vast Sandhills are the perfect backdrop for this subtle
drama."      —*Booklist*

"[An] emotionally rich first novel about an unwed pregnant teen
spending the summer with her grandmother in the hardscrab-
ble Nebraska Sandhills. . . . Her visit stirs up long-simmering
tensions for Toby, Toby's bitter sister Gertie, and George, who
has worked on the farm for more than 50 years. Seventy-two
and long widowed, Toby is no fawning grandma. Tough but loving, she still rides her horse regularly and can work up a man's
passions. . . . [George's] unspoken love makes for irresistible
reading. . . . Think Paul Newman with Joanne Woodward. . . .
A resonant love story, whatever the age of the lovers."
      —*Kirkus Reviews*

"Joern is particularly skilled at depicting contemporary small-town life and the issues rural communities face: the difficulty small farmers and ranchers have staying afloat financially and the decision of younger generations either to leave for urban areas or to endure directionless lives. She packs a lot of story into 250 pages."     —*Library Journal*

"*The Floor of the Sky* honors the pleasures and pitfalls of family without a shred of sentimentality. . . . [Joern] is a fine writer incapable of excess or artifice. Written in present tense, the book has an unintentionally cinematic quality. Its dialogue is varied and authentic. . . . A quiet little gem."
          —Pamela Miller, *Minneapolis Star-Tribune*

"Like Haruf's *Plainsong*, Joern's novel also makes good use of the setting—the stark Nebraska Sandhills, a blank slate devoid of trees and rain but also, seemingly, of the types of mysteries and scandals that might complicate the lives of city-dwellers. . . . Joern's prose is as clean as her landscape, and she paces the novel well, unraveling, one at a time, the small mysteries that keep the story moving along."
          —*Iron Horse Literary Review*

"*The Floor of the Sky* is a true gem of the storyteller's art, written with great compassion, wit and wisdom about the human condition, family secrets, and the sweeping changes in a contemporary rural America."
          —*Midwest Book Review*

"Pamela Carter Joern writes with compassion and a wry sense of humor, in a direct and true style that takes in the vivid details of the world of the Nebraska Sandhills and the complexities and nuances of her characters' inner lives. Her work may bring to mind the novels of Kent Haruf and Larry McMurtry—though, like the fiercely independent women that populate her novel, Joern is clearly an original!"

—Dan Chaon, author of *You Remind Me of Me*

"A testimony to the power of family secrets and the enduring legacy of the land."

—Mary Clearman Blew, author of
*Balsamroot: A Memoir*

"[Joern] is a fearless teller of hard truth. Set in the Sandhills of Nebraska, *The Floor of the Sky* is a tale of quiet heroics, a story of tenacity and courage, an intimate glimpse into the lives of independent ranchers determined to survive. A powerful portrayal of family, land, and loyalty. We are the wiser for having read it."

—Sheila O'Connor, author of *Where No Gods Came* and *Tokens of Grace*

"[Joern's] characters are sensible, endearing, and deeply haunted, and there's enough story and intrigue for ten novels. Secrets, old and new, keep the past constantly bumping into the present, making for a mesmerizing family saga."

—Timothy Schaffert, author of *The Singing and Dancing Daughters of God*

# THE PLAIN

**Flyover Fiction** | Series editor, Ron Hansen

**University of Nebraska Press** | Lincoln and London

Pamela Carter Joern

# SENSE OF THINGS

Library of Congress Catalog-
ing-in-Publication Data
Joern, Pamela Carter, 1948–
The plain sense of things /
Pamela Carter Joern.
    p. cm.— (Flyover fiction)
ISBN 978-0-8032-1619-8
(pbk.: alk. paper)
1. Nebraska—Fiction.
2. Domestic fiction. I. Title.
PS3610.O25P55 2008
813'.6—dc22
2008004002

Set in Granjon.
Designed by A. Shahan.

For my parents

After the leaves have fallen, we return
To a plain sense of things.

WALLACE STEVENS *The Plain Sense of Things*, 1950

# CONTENTS

# ACKNOWLEDGMENTS

First, to Brad, with love and gratitude. To Shannon and Matt, Raegan and Jacob, for filling my life with joy and possibility. To my friends—you know who you are—for constancy, caring, and good company. To the Hamline MFA program where the seeds of this book began. To Mary Rockcastle and Sheila O'Connor who believed in these stories from the beginning. To Paulette Bates Alden who encouraged me when I most needed it. To Greg Kosmicki who gently counseled that I might want to rethink the final chapter of an earlier version. To Tim Reckmeyer, for technical assistance. To Robert Carter, for creating my Web site. To Ladette Randolph and the crew at the University of Nebraska Press who have made this publishing process rewarding.

To my extended family—aunts and uncles, cousins, Bob

and Norma, Kent and Leania, nieces and nephews and their children, my stepdad Del, Margaret Joern, and all the other Mundts and Joerns whom I gained by marriage, and especially my parents, Marjorie Carter Caswell and Arthur Carter, to whom this book is dedicated—for giving me heroes, large and small.

Two of these stories were first published elsewhere. "Ghost Town" was published in *Laurel Review*, Winter 2005. Different versions of "Wonderful Words of Life" appeared in *Feminist Studies*, Summer 2003, and in *Times of Sorrow, Times of Grace: Writing by Women of the Great Plains/High Plains*, edited by Marjorie Saiser, Greg Kosmicki, and Lisa Sandlin (Omaha: The Backwaters Press, 2002).

I am haunted by the landscape of my childhood, and by landscape I mean both geography and the culture that has developed in response to it. Driving through a portion of western Nebraska on a bleak day in March, my husband once said: It takes something formidable to survive out here. Without much thought, I answered: Integrity and stubbornness. To all those whose stories spin out on the Plains, I salute you.

# THE PLAIN SENSE OF THINGS

# GHOST TOWN

GRAMP, 1930

Gramp went to fetch Billy himself after the telegram arrived announcing that Carlene had died. Grandma took to her bed, turned her face to the rose patterned wallpaper. Gramp sat at her back, careful not to mar her Double Wedding Ring quilt, tentatively reached his hand out toward his wife but could not think what to offer. He shrugged his shoulders, stood, said well then, and clumped off to the Elmyra train station.

See, he stands on the brick platform with his sheepskin jacket pulled snug against the wind. His shoulders sag. Metal clasps clang against a flagpole, the ground bare with scattered piles of dirty snow. His breath freezes in front of his face. It's early, the light gray and diffused. His jaw aches, clamped in anger.

The train *shuff-shuffs* onto the platform, and Gramp heaves himself up the steps to the passenger car. He's gotten heavy, his wavy hair white, his lower lip scarred from the cancer Dr. Blackford cut away. He still chews tobacco, a stolen pleasure when he's out in the barn or at the far end of the hayfield, brown juice dribbling through his ruined lip onto his overalls front so that he fools no one.

A private man, he moves to an empty seat. He settles into the worn velvet cushion and turns his head to watch the Nebraska prairie roll by. Later, after the train has passed through Cheyenne and Greeley, he steps out to take a breath of air. He's had no lunch, couldn't force a bite between his clenched teeth. His stomach is a bit off. He rides a while on the back end of the train, watching the track slide out from under the caboose and spin across the snowy ground. He'd made his way to this eastern plateau of Colorado as a young man. Orphaned at fifteen, he left England on a freighter and worked his way west from New York City to land a job in a candy factory. Every day he swept, mopped, toted bags of sugar, and every night at closing he scooped up what had spilled during the day and returned it to the swirling vats. He will never, for the rest of his life, eat a piece of store-bought candy, although he loves sweets and orders a dozen tins of fruitcake every Christmas.

The train rocks and rumbles, and although he is shivering and his hands are thrust deep in his pockets and the icy air sears his nostrils, he cannot bring himself to move back inside. He hates cramped spaces. He's thinking that if this had to happen, it's a good thing it happened in February when there's less work to be done in the fields.

After Fort Morgan, he leaves the train at Brush. He asks at the ticket window if anybody knows someone who might be driving south toward Heartstrong. He's told to inquire at the hardware store for Sal Hardy.

Amidst creaky wooden floors, air littered with sawdust, bins of nuts and screws, piled up lumber, pickles in a barrel, smells of oil and wood shavings and tinges of metal, he finds Sal Hardy, a runt of a man sitting on a pine chair tipped back into the corner. Old timer with nothing else to do.

"Hear you might be driving on out to Heartstrong after while."

Sal turns and studies him. "Could be." His voice grates like sand underfoot.

"I can pay."

Sal wipes a grizzled hand across his lower jaw. His long beard hangs in tufts like the mane of a wild mustang. His empty left sleeve pinned back against a shoulder stump.

"You got family there?"

"Some business to take care of."

"Business? Ain't no business in Heartstrong. Nobody left there but us ghosts." The old man laughs then, a silent tremor that shakes his body like a rug on the line.

Gramp stands his ground and lets the old man wind down. He offers no further explanation.

"Suit yourself." The old man shrugs. "I'm going that way anyhow."

Sal owns an old truck, the dashboard covered with chaws of spit-out tobacco. Gramp settles into the shotgun seat, places his feet carefully on either side of a gaping hole in the floorboard. He rides with his arms folded, not wanting to take up more space than he has to. Not wanting to touch anything.

The old man drives like a rough rider, yanking the truck with his good hand from one side of the road to the other in pursuit of a strip down the middle. There's no traffic to speak of. They pass one vehicle, horses hauling a farm wagon loaded with winter hay, and the driver gives the old man's truck a wide berth.

Gramp feels nothing for this ride or this old man. Dust and gravel and bits of ice spit up through the hole in the floor. He doesn't move a hand to wipe away the chips that dot his face.

When they reach Heartstrong, Gramp asks Sal to drop him in the center of town. Sal won't take his money, says he enjoyed the company. Says he makes the trip every day into Brush, that's his grandson owns the hardware store, so if Gramp needs a ride back, he can catch him on the corner about 10:00. Gramp thanks him, but promises nothing. He can't think of the boy riding in this old truck, his feet dangling precariously over the hole to the open road.

The business street of Heartstrong is four blocks long, a few side streets ambling off of that. The late afternoon light slants, pink tinges on the western edge. Gramp takes the telegram out of his pocket and reads the address again. Carlene's neighbor sent it, and she's got Billy there with her. He walks the streets of the town until he locates what he thinks must be the neighbor's house. Next door, a tiny shack sits back from the street, board planks laid across the front yard. Although the ground is frozen now, it must be a mudhole in summer, the way the house is sunk down low. It's ramshackle, all right, needing paint, tipped to one side. No curtains hang in the window. A padlock on the front door.

A woman steps out onto the porch of the neighbor's house. "You looking for Carlene?" she calls.

He waves the telegram at her. "I'm Carlene's father. Come for the boy."

The woman does not move and a space opens up between them, long enough for Gramp to know she's none too happy to see him. Then, she thrusts the door open. "Best you come on in here, then."

Her name is Melissa Carpenter, she's a spinster schoolteacher, and she has Billy sitting at the supper table, a napkin tucked into his shirt collar. In front of him, a plate of stew he's hardly touched.

"You eaten?"

Gramp shakes his head.

"Sit on down, then. Maybe you can get Billy to eat something."

She fusses around them, the man and the boy. She brings him coffee and a plate of stew and hot corn bread. She's homely, a spare frame draped by a brown flowered dress, her hair mouse-colored and twisted into a braid. She's been teaching school a while, he can see that. After putting his food on the table, she leaves the kitchen and goes off somewhere in the house. He hears her feet on the stairs.

He butters his corn bread, scoops stew into his mouth. He's aware the boy is watching him. He's a long, scraggly kid, his hair needing cut, hanging brown and limp. The kid's hands are knotted in his lap. He hardly moves, except for his eyes which are big and dark and full of sadness.

"My momma said you don't give a good goddamn what happens to us."

Gramp stops chewing and considers. He's shocked at such language from a kid, but then, what should he expect?

"You know who I am, then?"

The boy nods his head.

"We'll be going home to Elmyra in the morning."

The boy looks straight out into space. "No, sir. My momma's coming home. Like she always does."

Gramp washes his corn bread down with a swig of coffee. "Your momma left you home alone a lot?"

The boy shrugs. "When she's working."

"Where did she work?"

"Downtown. Flipping pancakes and burgers. I know how to get there. I can walk by myself in the park. I'm her big boy."

"You're kind of an old kid, aren't you?"

The boy doesn't answer. He sits perfectly still.

"Well, Old Kid, your momma's not coming home."

Gramp leans over his plate and softens his voice.

"She got sick, and then she died."

The kid starts yelling. He's up on his knees, his voice caterwauling, and then he's running around the kitchen. He's a bomb gone off, and Gramp puts out a hand to stop him when Melissa Carpenter flies around the doorway and catches the sobbing child in her arms. She kneels down to the boy and glares at Gramp over the boy's tousled head.

"What did you say to him?"

Gramp doesn't answer. He owes this woman nothing.

"Let me go, god dammit, let me go!" Billy struggles in Melissa's arms until she releases him. He races from the room, up the stairs, and a door slams.

Melissa Carpenter stands up and smoothes her skirt. "Mr. Preston. Why don't we sit down?"

"You should have told him."

"I did tell him. He's only five years old. He doesn't understand death."

Gramp moves through the front room, takes his coat from the rack and slides his arms into the sleeves. Melissa Carpenter closes in on him.

"Mr. Preston, we need to talk."

"Thank you for the supper."

"Don't you want to know where her body is?"

His hands fumble with the buttons of his coat, his fingers big and awkward. "I got to go."

"Where?"

"There must be a hotel downtown."

"You're wrong."

"Maybe. But that's for me to say."

"I mean about the hotel. Burned down last summer."

Gramp takes in this news and looks down at his boots. It's damn cold to sleep on the street. He won't ask this woman, even though she must have a room up those stairs.

"I got the key to Carlene's. You could sleep there."

She holds out a key swinging from a piece of cardboard. He's seen that look in her eye before. He's watched it over poker tables or during branding when nobody wants to take on the wildest calf. He saw it on the face of the stowaway who tried to steal his pack, the doctor who leaned over him when he lay weak and puking in his bunk, the parade of hustlers on his way west who thought they were dealing with nothing but a kid. He reaches his hand out for the key and does not look away from her stare.

"All right."

"There's an old oil stove in the living room. You'll have to light it."

"I expect I can manage. I'll be back in the morning for the boy."

"Billy. Billy is the boy's name. And he doesn't want to go home with you. He doesn't know you. I've known him almost three years. I looked after him, some."

She pulls herself up, then. She says the next line straight out, not like she's pleading for anything. "I want to keep him."

Gramp stops and grips his hat in his hands. He turns to gaze around Miss Carpenter's home, takes in her books, the piano, the embroidery-work lying on the rocking chair, stitches neat and tidy but the colors off, wholesome like everything else about her, and still you don't want any of it.

"I thank you for all you done. But that boy's mother is not coming back. And he don't belong to you."

He wrestles the padlock open without too much trouble. He leaves the door ajar so the moonlight can direct him. There's a kerosene lamp on a small table right of the front door. He feels around the top of the table for matches. He can't locate any and is thinking he'll have to grope his way to the kitchen when he bumps his head on a high shelf on the wall. He runs his hand along the shelf, what do you know, she's kept them out of reach of the boy.

After lighting the lamp, he shuts the door and turns to survey the tiny house. There's a shabby brown sofa with one of his wife's quilts covering it. He walks over and picks up the quilt, studies it to see how old it is, to see if his wife has defied him and sent this to Carlene or if it's something Carlene had since she was a girl. His fury mounts as he thinks of his wife sneaking behind his back. Too late, he's asked to pick up the pieces. Too late.

He's standing with the quilt balled in his fist. He doesn't want to think about his wayward daughter, her trampish ways. She had a string of good-for-nothing men in her short life. He's not even sure who Billy's father is. Not the married man they'd sent her here to get her away from. Not that namby-pamby boy cousin she married for four months before they had that marriage annulled. Not the second husband, either, that Wayne who'd married her pregnant and then left her when Billy was but a year old. He looks down at the pattern of blue and white, slows his breathing. He folds the quilt carefully and lays it back on the sofa, thinking he'll pack it up and take it home. He'll hand it to his wife and see what lie she spins this time.

He notices, now, the rest of the sparsely furnished room. There's a battered chair, the upholstery torn on one arm and white stuffing poking out. A pile of magazines. On one wall an embroidered plaque, Home Sweet Home, rough pink letters on a tan background, something Carlene must have done while learning at her mother's side. The floor is worn linoleum, but it's clean. An oil stove hunkers in a corner, the grated window dangling by one hinge. It's cold in the house, but not unbearable. He decides he'll do without the heat. He can see that the smoke has stained up the corner. The whole house smells of something, mold maybe, musty from being closed up, or there's a leak in the ventilation pipe.

Over a jagged threshold, he steps into the kitchen. An old wood stove, a pile of tinder in a rough wood box, a little table with one chair and a stool, a tiny cupboard painted with white enamel. A makeshift washstand, crates stacked and skirted with a rough-cut piece of green calico tacked to the edge. An empty bucket and dipper, a chipped enamel washpan. A small ice box in one corner. He looks out the window in the back door and spots an outhouse. Most of the snow has melted, leaving the ground dry and brown. Clouds block the moon, so he can't see where a pump might be.

He opens the little cupboard: three plates, three glasses, a couple of chipped cups, a few mismatched bowls. On the lower shelves, he finds canned beans and plums, rice, a bit of flour and sugar and salt and pepper. He opens the drawers one at a time, silverware, a couple of knives, some mixing spoons, in the bottom drawer a set of worn but finely embroidered tea towels. He picks up the top one, *Monday's child is fair of face*, recognizes his wife's work, lays it back in the drawer.

There's only one bedroom, the boy's cot against a wall, a double bed. Over the doorway she's hung a striped curtain, green and tan. He's guessing that when she had male visitors, she put the boy out on the sofa. Christ. There's one dresser, a second kerosene lamp on top. He takes the time to go back to the living room for matches and lights it. He pockets the matches. The lantern shade throws shadows on the wall, eerie spidery things, illuminating parts of the room and making the dark corners seem darker. He knows it's only tricks of light.

The top dresser drawer holds a few woman's underthings, the next two drawers the boy's clothes. Her clothes on hangers inside an old wardrobe. His hand brushes against a shiny, burgundy satin shimmy dress, and he recoils from it. Two hats, one with a rhinestone pin, on pegs inside the wardrobe.

He stands for several minutes and looks at the bed. It's piled high with blankets, and he's tired. He can't remember, now, if anybody said whether Carlene actually died in this room. He fumbles in his pocket for the telegram, torn and yellowed. He holds it in the lamplight and reads it over, but it says only that Carlene died of double pneumonia, two nights before last. He stares at the bed, thinking of the curtain over the doorway, trying not to imagine his daughter's white arms thrown back against the pillow.

He rumbles into the living room and tests out the sofa. A sharp spring has broken through the upholstery. He sweeps up the quilt, the one his wife made, and carries it to the boy's cot. He'll lie down here. This is good enough.

When he turns off the kerosene lamp in the living room, he realizes that it's not on a table at all, but on an upturned orange crate. He can use that for packing the boy's things. He supposed she'd have something here, a valise, a carpetbag, a brown paper sack, but there's nothing.

He stops, then, to listen. He doesn't believe in ghosts. He's not sure what he thinks about spirits or heaven. To him, when you're dead, you're dead, although he wouldn't tell anybody that. Let them have their comforts. He stops to listen out of curiosity and because, by god, if there is something waiting for him in this house, he intends to meet it head on. He strains in the semi-darkness, leans into it, but hears nothing.

After turning out the lamp, he hauls the orange crate into the bedroom. He lifts the boy's clothes out of the drawers and places them in half the partitioned crate. Maybe the rest of his things are over at Melissa Carpenter's. Surely a boy has a bit more than this to register his place on this earth. Surely he has a wooden truck. Or boots. Or flannel pajamas. More than these three pairs of patched pants and two worn shirts, a few scrabbledy pairs of socks and dingy underwear.

He won't take Carlene's things. Melissa Carpenter can have them. Sell them, if she wants, and keep the money. He doesn't want to touch his daughter's clothes.

He sits on the edge of the boy's cot to think. The eerie shadows sway, it's her clothes hanging, that fringed shawl, he knows it, and yet, the shadows bump him with their tendrils, stab at him like barbed wire. He'd supposed she had more than this. He'd always supposed somehow she managed, he didn't like to think how, but he knows he pictured her being taken care of by some man who had no right to her. There is that satin shimmy dress. Those hats. One thin curtain over the doorway between her bed and the living room.

He notices, then, a box tucked away underneath her bed. He can just spot the edge of it and he leans down to pull it forward. Inside, there is a wrapped form. A blanket shrouding something. He feels a clutch in his chest. He bolts from the room and stands trembling in the darkened living room, one thin sliver of moonlight knifing across the cold linoleum floor. He lays his hand on his chest to calm himself and considers the malice of Melissa Carpenter. She sent him over here, didn't she, with this key. She planned this for him, this announcement of Carlene's death, this final evidence of her ruined life.

He steels himself to go back. He holds his body far away while his hand reaches out to lift the blanket. He pulls it back to reveal a perfectly formed head, porcelain skin, bright blue eyes, actual hair glued on. It's only a doll, and he laughs out loud. The sound of his laughter echoes off the shadowed walls, fills him with relief and rings back to him with accusation. He passes a hand over his eyes and sits on the edge of the cot.

He lifts out the doll, finally, and recognizes her. She's one of two he brought from Cheyenne long ago when he'd had to work in the feed yards through the winter. He'd brought them to Mary and Carlene for Christmas. The girls had kissed his cheek and danced up and down, bobbing in the flickering candlelight from the Christmas tree.

Carlene's doll is perfectly preserved, her papier-mâché body still intact with ropes at the hinges. She wears a rose dress, a tucked bodice, glass rose buttons. He lifts the skirt and sees the ivory satin slip trimmed in lace, the little pantaloons. Her bonnet matches, the brim double layered. All tucks and pleats and buttons and lace, the way he thinks a girl should look, perfect and innocent, before her life gives way to aprons and lace-up oxfords.

He lays the doll on the bed. She looks cold and lonesome, and he folds the edge of his wife's quilt over her. He tucks it around her face, holds her curved fingers in his large bungling hand. He decides to leave the lamp burning and he lies down on the boy's cot, careful not to disturb the doll, and he waits through a sleepless night for morning.

Melissa Carpenter gives him breakfast, a fine meal of eggs and bacon and fried potatoes. She says almost nothing, but she has talked to the boy. Gramp notices that the boy eats a bit of his food and takes that as a good sign.

Melissa sends the boy upstairs for his things, a few articles of clothing packed in a bag she has provided. When he's gone, she turns away from Gramp and looks out over her frozen yard.

"She wasn't sick long. She just came down with it, and before anybody knew, it went to her lungs. She tried to keep working, too long, I guess. Worried about Billy. She was always worried about Billy and how she'd get enough money."

Melissa's hand fumbles in her dress pocket for a handkerchief. She presses it to her face and keeps on talking. Gramp cannot take his eyes from the set of her shoulders.

"Dr. Carrington sent her to the hospital in Brush. The last couple of days. She didn't die alone. Billy was here with me, but she had friends, and the nurses, too. She just slipped off, Doc said. Like sliding under water."

She turns and faces him. He says nothing, his throat clogged with something heavy and sharp. He's waiting for her to denounce him, braced for her anger. He thinks of a branding iron, the hot steam rising from seared flesh, and he wants it, that cleansing. He can see she's got it rising inside her, hands clenched, teeth bared, her eyes hard and cold against him.

Something happens then, some change comes over her. He can't say why, maybe she just feels the futility of it all or decides she won't help him punish himself. He can't say whether it's kindness or defeat or a calculated aim, but she swallows whatever she had planned to say and substitutes a soft knife that cuts deep.

"Letters from home meant a lot to her. She'd read them to me most times. I know your wife makes those beautiful quilts, all those tiny stitches. I know you and Jake cut the harvest by hand. I know you moved Mary home when her husband died, built that little house for her and the two boys."

She stops, then. Billy has come down and is standing in the doorway. Gramp puts his hands on the edges of the table and hoists his leaden body to its feet. His hand reaches into his pocket and drags out his metal-clasped pocketbook. His clumsy fingers snap it open and retrieve a five-dollar bill, the one he's been saving for months tucked under his mattress. He watches his arm extend and hold the money out to Melissa Carpenter. He wonders if his voice will hold up, and then he opens his mouth to test it.

"If you wouldn't mind, I'd ask you to see to it that Carlene's body is sent home to Elmyra. I think she should be where the boy can visit."

Melissa Carpenter nods her head. She takes the money.

"If there's more money needed, I'll wire it. If there's anything you want in the house . . ." He stops, presses his lips together and draws in a sharp breath.

Melissa Carpenter waves her hand. She presses her handkerchief against her mouth, her face bunched up. Gramp nods and fumbles his pocketbook back into his overalls.

The boy is standing by the packed orange crate. Gramp puts his hand on the back of the boy's head and nudges him toward Melissa. "Go on, Old Kid. Say your good-byes."

She enfolds him, then kneels to look him in the eye. "You make your mother proud, you hear?"

"Yes, ma'am."

The boy picks up his packed bag. Gramp hefts the orange crate. The doll was too long to fit inside the partitioned crate, so Gramp has wrapped her in his wife's quilt and laid her on top. Underneath the doll is the carefully folded satin shimmy dress and the hat with rhinestones. He tucks the whole parcel under one arm and reaches down to rest his other hand on the boy's shoulder as they make their way down town to meet Sal Hardy. Gramp's already planning how he'll hold the boy on his lap so he won't be frightened by the hole in the floor of Sal's truck. He'll hold him all the way to Brush, and then they'll be all right.

# HARD TIMES AHEAD

MARY, 1935–1937

### The Funeral

Mary Cuzak watches her second husband's coffin lowered into the ground. She presses her hand against the small of her back to counter the pendulous weight of her pregnant belly. Her feet hurt in rundown shoes. She turns her mind from the reverend's droning voice. She can't wait to get her feet up, eat a little cake.

Look at Alice. Huddled at the foot of her father's grave. Of his four big children, Alice was her father's favorite. Mary saw how he bragged on Alice's good nature, ruffled her curly hair when he should have been tossing Ruth, their own baby, over his shoulder. He made no end of excuses for those three big girls, letting them run wild in the raspberry canes. Their brother Edward, typical, stands there like a scarecrow, arms stiff at his sides.

The baby presses on Mary's sciatica. She drops Ruth's hand, reaches around her to tap Timmy on the shoulder. He's cutting up with Nick, the way boys do. She thought they'd mind better once she married Richard, but he'd never taken to them. She'd met him when he walked down the road a half mile to the Preston place and hired her to bake bread for his family. She was living a widow's life, two small boys, and he was lonely with a houseful of children needing looked after. She'd had no idea, none.

She's a young woman, barely thirty, but life gets away from her. The minister throws dirt on the coffin. His black-clothed arm stretches and dry clods thump on the wooden lid. Dust to dust. Sunlight darts in and out of the cottonwood leaves. Even if she puts her hand out, she knows she can't catch the sun.

Later, at Richard's brother's house, she wanders from room to room. William and his wife Luella are heartsick, but they're kind to her. William has a bald head and the biggest ears she's ever seen. She hopes the baby in her belly doesn't get those ears.

There are people here Mary's never met, relatives of Richard's first wife Pauline. Richard's four big children love the attention, they're basking in it. Mary supposes this is hard for them, only four years after their mother died. She can't help that. They'll have to get used to it, the way she's had to get used to a lot of things.

Mary roams, looking for a chair, a wall to lean on. Her own people didn't make the trip from Elmyra to North Platte. This is home for Richard. He's resting finally beside his dead first wife. Mary's a stranger here.

Through a lace-curtained window, she sees Edward standing by a lilac hedge, his hands shoved deep in his pockets. She sizes him up, trying to figure if he's man enough to keep the farm going. She can't see it. Almost planting time, and she can't think past getting this baby out and being able to see her feet.

Two women stand by the parlor piano. One of them wears a black hat with feathers. The other waves her hand in front of her face when she talks. Pauline's sisters, Mary believes, although no one has introduced her. They have those big Bohemian eyes, like pictures she's seen of Pauline. Mary fingers the buttons at the neck of her shapeless black dress while she listens.

"Poor Pauline. I'm glad she's not here to go through this."

"They say he screamed so loud the nurses had to put him off in the basement, away from the other patients."

Mary turns away from their voices. She doesn't want to know what the doctors did to him. They shoot horses with a broken leg, but a man with a broken neck is made to suffer. Fall off a haystack in the prime of your life, they haul you across the state to a university hospital, away from your wife and children, where they put you in a basement because they can't stand to hear you scream.

"It was no picnic for us either," Mary blurts out. She hopes to shame the two women at the piano into thinking about her. She wants them to picture her through the long winter months, pregnant, seven children, in another woman's house. She knows they don't have the imagination for it. Their minds are stuck in that hospital, listening to phantom screams of a dying man and thinking of his dead wife who doesn't have a care in this world.

Lunch is laid out on the dining room table. Sandwiches, potato salad, oatmeal cookies, a chocolate cake. A punch bowl with little glass cups. Mary doesn't want anything to eat, but she can't stop looking at that table. Silver spoons fanned out, sugar in a china bowl with a lid. She overhears a phrase here, there, *depression, the president, unemployment*. She lays her fingers on a damask napkin as one man says *we all have to make sacrifices*.

A tall woman dressed in black and white polka dots walks toward her. She wears high-heeled shoes and silk stockings. A man in a gray suit follows behind her.

"I'm Norah," the woman says. "And this is Henry, Pauline's brother."

Mary nods, but says nothing. Her feet are killing her now. This man has normal ears, does that matter? She's having trouble keeping all the bloodlines straight.

"We'd like to talk to you." Norah delivers this as an order.

"All right." Mary is surprised to hear her own voice. It sounds hard, like something scraped against the woodshed.

"In the parlor." Norah turns on her pricey shoes and takes a step.

"Right here will be just fine." Mary leans against the doorjamb, her pregnant profile blocking the doorway.

Norah steals a look at Henry. She arches her eyebrows, and Henry takes over.

"I'll come right to the point." Henry's voice is soft. He has nice brown eyes, and Mary almost forgets to be careful. "We want Alice to live with us. For a while. Let her go to school in Paxton."

"What about Libby and Grace?" Mary asks. What she means is, why not take all three of them?

"I know they'll miss her." Norah's turn now. "But Alice is starting her junior year of high school this fall, and that will be a critical time for her. Grace needs to finish out there in Elmyra because she's graduating. And Libby won't even be in high school yet."

Mary tries her best to follow this reasoning. They want Alice. Everybody always wants Alice. It would be one less mouth for her to worry about, but then, she'd have less help, too. Grace is a good worker, but she has to be told everything.

"She can't go this summer. Not with all the work that needs doing."

Norah all but claps her hands. "We've thought of that. We'll come in August and pick her up. That way we can look in on all of you."

"Check up on us, you mean?"

Norah starts to say something, but clamps her lips together. Mary turns her head away from them. She knows if she waits long enough, when she turns back they'll be gone. This whole family disappears like ghosts.

The big girls are standing at the dining room table, laughing and picking at the cake. Alice's dark curls fly around her face. Grace has a startled look, like she sees hard times ahead. Libby's hand clutches Alice's skirt. Mary watches them for a while. Then she quietly walks up behind them, reaches out and pinches Alice's thigh, hard.

"Ow!" Alice turns. She sputters until she sees Mary. Her eyes grow wide and she takes a small step back. "Why'd you do that?"

Mary waits for her to cry, but Alice doesn't. Mary stares at Alice trying to see what everybody else sees in her. Must be this, Mary thinks. Must be that she can look straight back at me and not cry on the day of her daddy's funeral.

"You go on, now." Mary tosses her head in the direction of the door. "You girls get on out of here. Leave this room for the adults."

After the girls skitter out the door, Mary finds herself alone. She takes in the Rose O Sharon patterned glass on the table. Runs her eyes up the blue latticed wallpaper. On the oak sideboard, a framed picture of William and Luella with their three children. There's something about the faces that looks off to Mary. They look happy and unnatural, and while she is pondering what that means, her hand reaches out, grabs a silver spoon and drops it into her dress pocket.

## The Courtship

A year later, on a Sunday afternoon, Mary sits at her kitchen table snapping beans. Libby's got Ruth outside dangling her feet in the horse tank, Edward's checking on the cattle in the south pasture, and Helen is down for a nap. Timmy and Nick walked to Pumpkin Creek with their fishing poles. Grace is hovering over the cook stove and worrying about whether her rice pudding will set up right. Mary has shown her a dozen times how to do it, but Grace doesn't have the knack.

Mary reaches out and pushes the pile of beans in Grace's direction. "You might as well make yourself useful while you're waiting. Watching it like a hawk won't make a bit of difference."

Grace bites her lip and plops in a chair across from Mary at the wooden table. Her light brown hair frizzes at the temples from the heat in the kitchen. Studying her, Mary thinks again that Grace probably needs glasses, but there's no money.

"I don't see why he's sniffing around here. You girls are way too young for him."

Mary's talking about her brother Jake who farms with their father on leased land a half mile up the road. He's got Alice out riding in his truck, bumping over washboard roads on a Sunday afternoon in the full heat of summer.

Grace doesn't answer. Mary might as well talk to the wall. Mary looks out the window, her hands busy with the beans, and takes in the dirt yard, the drying grapevines, the tilting vane on the roof of the barn.

"We don't get rain soon," Mary says, "that corn won't be fit to harvest. Beans, either."

Still Grace says nothing. Mary knows now it was a mistake to let Alice go away last fall to Paxton. Libby cried herself to sleep most nights. With the new baby, the indoors work fell to Grace.

Mary'd had to slap Grace a couple of times. She'd knuckled under and gotten things done, but she'd fallen silent.

Mary sets her thin lips in a tight line and snaps beans faster. "You can stop feeling sorry for yourself, Grace. There's not enough sorry to go around for all of us."

Grace shifts her feet under the table. She can't just drop the beans into the pot, she has to toss every snapped bean so that it chimes against the metal.

"Stop that."

"What?" There. Mary finally has Grace's attention.

"Stop that racket."

Grace takes to piling the snapped beans on the table in front of her. She waits until she has a little pile accumulated and then cradles the beans with her two hands and gently lays them in the pot. All the while she does this, she glares at Mary.

Mary wipes the back of her neck with a handkerchief from her apron pocket. "They should be back by now."

"Why'd you let her go?" Grace says this with a sullen attitude, but at least she's talking.

"You're just mad because he didn't ask you."

"I don't want some old hayseed farmer."

Mary says nothing for a while. The wrong people fall in love. Young men die. The mortgage payments are due. The harvest looks meager. These beans have blight. "Want don't have much to do with most things," she says.

### The Baptism

The next spring, on the morning of Alice's baptism, Mary finds that she cannot get out of bed. Her back aches more than usual. Helen is still asleep in her crib. Ruth has scooped herself off the cot, dragged her blanket by a corner, and sprawled across Mary's feet. Mary can hear the big girls clanging in the kitchen. She knows any minute Helen will wake up. The big girls squabble with Timmy and Nick, tell them to wash their ears, don't hog all the biscuits, stop feeding Ginger beneath the table.

There's something dark and heavy sitting behind Mary's eyes. It's the end of April and the work just piles up. Planting, milking, the garden to cultivate, the raspberries picked and jellied, spring cleaning. The desk in the front parlor chock full of unpaid bills. Mary lifts her hand and holds it in front of her face, moves her fingers apart and together, makes patterns against the glow of the window.

It's too much, Mary thinks. Ruth stirs and climbs down off Mary's bed. She stands with her thumb in her mouth, her blanket wadded up under her arm. Mary tucks a stray hair behind Ruth's ear and then gently pushes her toward the door.

When Helen wakes and cries, Mary pushes herself up on one elbow. "Grace," she yells. "Gra-a-ace."

Grace pushes open Mary's door. She stands on one foot, her round face tilted and eyes squinting. "Come get Helen," Mary says. She's so tired that she falls back on her pillow.

Grace sweeps Helen up and goes out. Mary can hear all the children now, clambering for water and milk and biscuits, shouting and demanding, *give me, give me*. She closes her eyes against them.

Later, a timid knock on the door. They've sent Libby. Clever. "Mary, aren't you coming?"

Sweet Libby. Little Libby. Mary does not roll over. She keeps her face to the wall.

Libby ventures closer and lays a hand on Mary's shoulder. Mary shudders at the touch. "Mary?"

"Edward can drive all of you."

"But it's Alice's baptism."

"Alice can get baptized without me being there."

Libby waits, but Mary knows she can outlast her. Soon, Libby will turn away and leave the room. Soon, she will hear the motor of the car. Then, they'll all be gone, and she can have peace and quiet. Alice will don her white robe, walk down the steps into the baptismal waters, take the Rev. Morris's hand and fall backward into burial with Jesus, and Mary will not rise from her dark sleep.

### The Graduation

Alice is graduating from high school, three weeks after her baptism and one month before her wedding. Mary has been agitated all day, waiting to get Jake alone to talk with him about her plan. She sent Helen and Ruth to nap, Timmy and Nick outside to feed the chickens. Edward's in the fields, of course, and Alice, Grace, and Libby are hoeing the garden. Jake stopped by with rolls Grandma Preston baked for the graduation party, and Mary has him to herself. She sits him down at the kitchen table and serves him coffee thick with sugar and cream the way he likes it. She talks fast.

"So, Jake." She catches herself wringing her hands. "What I was thinking is, you and Pop don't own that land. You know how Pop is, stubborn old Englishman who won't pay land tax. But I own this land. It's in my name, Richard left it to me when he died. Only I need somebody to work it. It's too much for Edward, and I can't afford to keep hiring help."

She waits for Jake to help her out. She waits for him to reach the same conclusion before she gets there. He says nothing.

"I know you and Alice plan to live with Mama and Pop. But you could live here. You could work this land, and I'd give you a share of it."

Jake sets his coffee cup on the table. He rubs his hand along his jaw. She sees now that he has a heavy crop of whiskers. He's got a broad forehead, wire-rimmed glasses and thin, wavy hair.

"What would Pop and Mama do?" Jake says.

Mary stands up. She takes the coffee pot off the stove and pours Jake a second cup. "I've thought of that. They could move here, too. We'd all be better off."

Jake clears his throat. He shifts his feet under the table. "You know Pop won't go for that."

"He would if you'd tell him. He wouldn't have a choice." She reaches across the table for his hand but pulls back before she touches him. "You got to look out for yourself, Jake. Pop won't be around forever, and if I lose this farm, none of us will have anything."

"Pop won't ever let you starve, Mary, you know that."

Mary stands. She walks to the window and stares outside. This is what she has been afraid of. Jake's complete confidence in their father. His inability to look ahead. She tries again. "Jake, without land, there's no security."

"Pop says land ties you down."

"Pop don't know everything."

Jake fidgets in his chair. "I don't see how I can leave Pop and Mama to themselves, Mary. Maybe I can try to help you out some. I plan to get a little place of my own, once I get ahead. This is your place. And besides, Alice needs a fresh start."

Mary sweeps Jake's cup up off the table. She swings open the screen door and flings the coffee dregs out into the yard. Ginger yelps when the scalding coffee catches her on the haunches.

Jake squares his shoulders and steps out into the yard. "Well, then," he says.

### The Wedding

On the day of Alice and Jake's wedding, Mary stands outside at dawn and watches the sun lick the sky red and gold. She's leaning on the garden gate, and she can smell the moist earth. Light falls on the blades of the windmill and shimmers with the lazy turning in the morning breeze. If she were a praying woman, she'd be praying now. Instead, she breathes in the quiet for a while before she straightens and turns to the house to meet the day.

Alice has picked the worst possible time for her wedding. Ten o'clock in the morning, so everybody has to scramble to get the chores done, wash up the separator, get through breakfast, scrub the kitchen floor. Libby is put in charge of the younger children. Mary shoves a broom into Grace's hand. "Just sweep off that parlor rug, we don't have time to take it outside and beat it."

Jake gets there, with Gramp and Grandma Preston and Billy who dashes off to find the boys. Grandma comes in the house and starts poking around the kitchen for something to do. Mary sets her to wiping off the dining room table. Jake and Gramp wander out by the Chinese elms.

At a quarter of ten, Rev. Morris drives in. Mary puts him in the front parlor and tells Edward to keep him company. The three big girls are off giggling in their room. Libby and Grace are helping Alice into the dress she ordered from the J.C. Penney's catalogue. Cream colored, cotton net lace, blue trim around bell-sleeves, a blue satin ribbon for a belt. It looks like a big christening gown to Mary, but it only cost three dollars, so what can you expect?

At five 'til, Mary still hasn't had time to change her clothes. She puts her hand on the doorknob to her room. She stops, draws in her breath, chews on her bottom lip. She flings open the door, drags her bibbed apron off over her head and tosses it on the bed. She checks her hair in the mirror above the bureau and tucks in a few loose strands. She smoothes her navy checked workdress over her hips, hollers at Ruth to stop wadding up her skirt and calls Grace to help get Helen dressed. "You'll have to do," she says to her reflection.

Grabbing her sewing shears from her top bureau drawer, she

runs outside. She races to the south side of the barn where two days ago she'd noticed some volunteer sweet peas. Some of them have fallen over in the wind, but she manages to cut several for a small bouquet. Pink and white, she raises them to her nose. She flies in the back door, remembering to catch the screen before it slams. Rev. Morris is standing in the parlor, his hands upon a Bible. Jake looks handsome in his brown suit. Gramp and Grandma have their hands full, taming Timmy and Nick who want to stick their fingers in the icing of the cake. Billy stands to one side, looking for all the world like he's at a funeral. Grace and Libby are sitting down, each one cradling one of the little girls on her lap, whispering in their ears, sh-h-h. Edward stands awkward and stiff as a poker behind his sisters' chairs.

Mary looks around frantically for Alice. Where is that girl? She has looked right past her. Alice is a statue in the doorway to the parlor. Hair waved back from her face, lips translucent and red, her slim figure outlined by the cheap wedding gown. Alice's eyes are locked on Jake as she steps forward to join him in front of Rev. Morris. Mary sees the naked hope and believes that Alice is nothing but a foolish girl, and yet, as she moves past, Mary stretches out her arm and hands off the bouquet of flowers.

# SLIDING DOWN THE MILKY WAY

LIBBY, 1937

Libby is sitting on the fence in the south pasture when Alice finds her. She's been there since early afternoon, feet propped on the lower split rail. The skirt of her summer cotton dress is tucked under her thighs, her dark hair tied back with a yellow ribbon. Libby doesn't turn her head when Alice snuggles up beside her. She's done with that. Besides, Alice has other things to tend to now that she's married.

"Hey, Libby." Libby used to like Alice's cheerfulness. She used to watch her flying hands and admire her curly hair.

"What're you doing out here all alone?"

Libby laughs inside herself. She's thinking Alice never could stand to be alone. Not for a single minute. Now look at her. Hooked to Jake for life.

"She's out there." Libby speaks from a dream. "Think of it, Alice. Alone out there. Just her and all that sky."

"No one's been able to find her. They said on the radio she must be down and that navigator with her."

"Fred Noonan."

"Who?"

"Amelia's navigator. Fred. That's his name. You'd know if you ever read the papers."

Libby watches Alice raise her hand to shield her eyes from the sun. Libby's looking straight west, toward the Pacific, and she doesn't care if the sun blinds her. Amelia flies straight into the sun. She has goggles, of course. She wears man's pants and a tie. She pulls a helmet on her head and doesn't care whether it smashes her hair or not. Fred sits behind and can't help falling in love with her. Amelia's married, but Fred can't help himself.

"You going to have a baby soon?" Libby asks this without looking at her sister. Alice is nuts about babies.

"Jake says I have to grow up first." Alice giggles. Libby doesn't join her.

"Well, when you do, I hope it's a girl, and I hope she flies around the world."

"Libby, you got to stop talking like this."

"Why's that?" Libby figures Alice is thinking of that other time, after Momma died. Libby pretended for months that Momma wasn't really gone. Libby almost laughs out loud when she thinks of the three of them, she and Alice and Grace all huddled in that bed together. Libby whispered *Good night, Momma*, and the other two acted as if they'd seen ghosts. She guessed she knew she was pretending. Although it did seem sometimes that if she tried hard enough, she could smell Momma's perfume. Taste her lip rouge. Smooth her hair between her fingers.

Libby hears Alice's voice from a distance. "You sitting out here mooning on this fence every afternoon. Don't you have something better to do?"

Libby turns and looks at her sister. "What would that be?"

"Come home with me." This is only about the hundredth time Alice has asked her. Alice lives up the road a half mile, at the Preston place. Every day since her wedding a month ago, she's walked down to talk to Libby, but Libby hasn't set foot in the Prestons' yard.

"Can't." Libby focuses on the sky. "I'm watching for Amelia."

A year ago, when Jake first started walking down to the home place, she and Alice laughed at him. Big ol' serious man. He wore overalls, work boots. His bottom teeth toppled together like gravestones in a country churchyard. Since Mary didn't act like a mother, no one thought of her brother Jake as family. And he was old. Thirty.

It got clear before long that Jake fancied Alice. He'd stand talking to her out by the pump. Catch her at the end of the lettuce rows and block off the path to the house. He took to bringing her little presents, a dog whittled out of wood, a peacock feather. Alice couldn't abide him. One day she and Libby climbed out the bedroom window and ran behind the chicken house to hide from him. He stood in the yard talking to Mary, scuffled his big-toed boots in the dirt, craned his neck to look this way and that. The girls put their hands over their mouths to stifle giggles and bumped their hips together watching around the side of the shed.

"You girls are awful to him." Grace accused them late at night.

Alice elbowed Libby in the ribs, and they set off in fits of laughter. That's the way they were, then, Libby and Alice, Alice and Libby. They left Grace out shamelessly.

In the twilight, they sat in the shadow of a haystack, legs flung out in front of them. Alice tugged on Libby's pigtail. Libby yelped, then laced her arm through Alice's, measured their hands palm to palm.

"We'll go to Hollywood."

"Paris. Let's do Paris tonight."

"Okay. Paris. What's in Paris?"

"French people?" Gales of laughter. Then, Libby began the game again.

"The Eiffel Tower."

"I'm afraid of heights."

"Don't worry. You won't have to climb it."

"Then don't you climb it either."

"Okay. But, I might. Climb it. I'll wave to you."

Things turned one day when Libby and Alice were feeding chickens in the yard. They made a game of it, tossing potato peelings in small handfuls to draw the chickens one way and then another. Chickens cackling, the girls giggling, timing their tosses to prove who made the best Pied Piper. Jake rolled in on that big Farmall, straight from the field. He stepped down, the tractor still running, took off his cap, wiped his forehead with a red bandanna he fished from his hip pocket. Libby looked at Alice, her feet already positioned to run and hide, but Alice was standing up straight, her head cocked to one side, a grin spreading on her face.

"Wonder if he'd let me drive that thing."

"Don't, Alice," Libby warned. Don't, don't, don't get too near.

But Alice walked over to Jake. She tilted her head up at him and asked if he'd show her how to drive. He hoisted her up on the seat, Alice's skirt hiking up over her knees. He demonstrated how to pull back the gear shift. Later, he swore he told her where to put her foot on the brake, but Alice said he didn't, and anyway, by then it was too late. Alice took the tractor around the yard a few turns before she began to get frightened. Libby and Jake, standing twenty feet apart, heard Alice shrieking, and then she aimed the tractor straight toward the side of the house. She said afterward that she couldn't think how else to stop. Jake leapt up behind her on the seat. It was impressive, Libby had to admit, the way he timed it, like roping a calf at the rodeo or running into a game of jump rope. He reached his strong arm over Alice's shoulder and gripped the wheel, turned the lumbering machine away from the house, and at the same time, slipped the key from the ignition. The tractor shuddered and stopped, and Libby watched while Alice gazed over her shoulder into the hazel eyes of the man who saved her. The man who stood as tall as their dead father.

In late July, Libby lies in her bed one night, her face turned to the wall. Grace sleeps on the other side, snoring softly after a long day of methodical work. Libby thinks about Amelia and Fred Noonan, lost only a few miles away from their destination. Earlier that day, the radio reported that a Coast Guard ship received calls from her, but for some reason Amelia could not hear their return messages, and Libby cannot imagine anything sadder, to be cut off like that, thinking no one cares. She tosses and turns, wishing Grace would talk to her, and, at the same time, hoping Grace doesn't waken. If she does, all she'll say is, Go to sleep, we've got work to do in the morning.

She and Alice used to talk about everything, whispering and giggling while Grace complained and threatened to push them both off onto the floor. Even when Alice talked about nothing but Jake, Libby tried not to mind. She liked some of the stories, especially the ones about how Jake would sing to Alice, put his voice low and throaty against her ear. It sent shivers down Libby's back to hear about that, but she never let on. To Alice, she said, "I bet he can't dance."

Libby tries to picture Alice with Jake. She sees them lying in bed together. She knows they do what married people do. After Alice and Jake got home from their honeymoon to Denver, she'd cornered Alice back of the machine shed. Alice was cutting wild goldenrod to hang and dry. She sat on the ground in a lilac dress, her skirt scattered around her, a big basket beside her half-filled with lacy, yellow plumes.

"Well," Libby said. "How was it?"

Alice kept on stuffing goldenrod into her basket. Libby tugged on her arm.

"C'mon, Alice. What was it like?"

"What was what like?"

"The hotel. Everything."

Libby watched Alice's eyes go soft, her lips tuck into a secret smile. "The hotel was dreamy. Big old bed, like that iron one Mary and Daddy had."

"So, what happened?"

"We got there." Alice kept on snipping goldenrod, not looking at Libby. "I took off my sailor blouse and hung it in the closet." She turned then, finally. "Actual closets, Libby. Not just a wardrobe."

"And then?"

Alice giggled a little. She sounded almost like her old self, and Libby started to relax. They fell into each other when Alice said, "I didn't know what to do." Libby could just picture it, Alice standing there in her chemise, big old clumsy Jake with his hat in his hands across the room. Oh, it was funny, too funny.

But then Alice sat up. She tidied her hair with her hands, picked up her basket to stand. Libby, still sitting on the ground, reached up and grabbed the hem of Alice's skirt.

"So, then what?"

Alice smiled down at her. The way Aunt Norah used to smile

at them after their mother died. The way Libby herself smiles at her little half-sisters when they ask a dumb question. "It was wonderful, Libby. That's all. Someday you'll find out for yourself."

Now, lying in bed, worried for Amelia and Fred, Libby wishes she could have Alice back the way it used to be. She can't fall asleep without Alice's hip next to hers. If she could just have Alice back until she nods off, then she wouldn't be so tired all the time.

When she does finally slip into sleep, it's fitful, and she dreams that she is sliding down the Milky Way when she spots an airplane in the distance. She calls out to Amelia, *come home, come home*, but she keeps on sliding, sliding farther away and Amelia doesn't hear her. She can't get off the Milky Way and Amelia doesn't hear her, and in the dream, it is she who disappears while Amelia flies on.

By mid-August, Alice has stopped walking down to the home place every day. One evening, after the stars are out, Libby climbs down from the rail fence in the south pasture. She walks through the sticky-sweet alfalfa along the windbreak. She hears crickets, an occasional owl. A full moon perches above her, like a sewn-on sequin.

She does not go up the lane to the Prestons' yard. Instead, she crosses the ditch, scrambles beneath a barbed wire fence and comes up behind the big house where Jake's parents live. Through the window she sees them sitting by lamplight. Gramp and Grandma Preston. Jake, too. Listening to the radio. Maybe the National Farm and Home Hour.

Libby hears laughter. She scuttles from behind the house to a large cottonwood tree. The bark scrapes thick and chunky against her palms. From there she views the whole yard, glowing in the moonlight. Down yonder sits the little house where Alice and Jake live, the house Mary and her two boys lived in before she came to be their stepmother. Alice has planted something in the window boxes, Libby can't make it out from this far away. Probably zinnias.

Libby hears laughter again, and Alice flies out from behind the barn. She's racing for her life and behind her tromps one of the Wilmington boys from up the road. Libby notices, then, an upturned can squatting on the ground. Alice reaches it first, stretches out her leg and sends it sailing through the night air. *Kick the Can*, she yells, and the boy groans in his defeat, and other kids emerge from hiding places. Nick and Timmy, Libby's stepbrothers, dart out from behind the garden fence. She shoots arrows into their hearts from this distance. They fall dead, and no one pays attention, especially Alice who is busy, after all, being a married woman. The other Wilmingtons appear, and somebody else, a girl Libby doesn't recognize, maybe a Wilmington cousin or a friend visiting from town. Billy, too, who's thirteen now, only four years younger than Alice.

The kids all crowd around Alice. They press against her, she's laughing and spinning, her hands held high in the air, her laughter bubbling and carrying them along until the whole group spirals and whirls, kids falling down right and left as if they are playing statue.

Libby doesn't move from behind the tree. Not until Jake comes out on the porch of the big house. He stands there, hands buried in his overalls pockets. By now, the kids have grown quieter. They're in a phase of deciding what to do next when Jake clears his throat.

"Gotta go," Alice says.

Jake steps down off the porch and Alice walks forward to meet him. She reaches out to take his hand. Together they move toward the little house. The other kids, spent from too much fun and lost without their leader, break up and start to move toward homes in opposite directions. Libby crouches deeper behind the tree, but she doesn't have to worry. Nick and Timmy move toward the lane to the road. She makes a break for it before Alice disappears into the house. She runs panting back the way she has come, under the barbed wire, through the ditch, along the windbreak, across the alfalfa field. Her breath comes out in gasps, and her side aches bad, and the moon shines on and on as if nothing has changed.

After that, Libby spies on Alice regularly. She hides behind a different tree each night. Once or twice, she risks going during the daytime, lurks behind the corner of the barn or crouches alongside the outhouse and watches Alice hang clothes on the line or sweep off her front step. Who is this new Alice? The tidy housekeeper? The child who comes out to play after supper, one night Kick-the-Can, the next a rousing game of Work-up? The married woman who disappears with her husband behind closed doors at bedtime? How is Libby supposed to know who she's talking to, when her sister is pretending to be all these different people?

One day, when she's hiding in the windbreak watching Alice scrub a tub full of clothes outside, she steps out from behind an elm tree. She's a long way away, fifty yards or more, but she dares Alice to look up at her. She doesn't wave or shout because if Alice thought of her at all, the way she used to, she'd feel Libby's presence, and she'd look up. But Alice doesn't even glance her way. Alice keeps on scrubbing clothes on an old washboard, and Libby walks home, kicking the dirt with her shoes.

She's stopped spying by the time Jake comes by one Saturday to help with the fall harvest. Libby's sitting on the front step cradling Ginger, a part collie, part golden retriever who's got something wrong with her paw. Libby has the big dog sprawled across her lap, trying to get a look at the paw, but Ginger's having none of it. She fights to get free, bangs her head around, smacks Libby in the face, and yelps like she's being tortured. It's all Libby can do to hang onto her.

Jake sits down on the front step next to Libby and the dog. He puts his hand on the dog's head.

"There, now," Jake croons. "There, there," and the dog whimpers. Ginger looks into Jake's face, and her tongue flicks out to lick him. Jake keeps on talking to her, and as long as his voice is going, Ginger lies quiet and docile. Libby manages to finger the paw, find an embedded stone and work it out.

"How'd you do that?" Libby asks. She doesn't look at Jake. She won't give him that much.

Jake nods. "I don't know. Animals like me, I guess. Always have."

They sit a spell longer. It's strange, this moment of quiet. Any minute Libby knows Ruth or Helen will come flying out the door, or Timmy and Nick will holler at each other across the yard. She's caught in this space with Jake, and she can see there's something still within him. He's restful.

"Well." Jake rises, brushes his cap against the leg of his overalls. "I best get to work while it's still daylight." He turns and looks in the direction of the Preston place, out over the windbreak, off down the road. He can't see Alice, but Libby feels his yearning.

"Alice gets mighty lonesome all day."

He's gone then, walking away, and it's a good thing, too, so he can't see Libby put her face down on Ginger's head, so he can't see her cry and cry.

A few days later that fall, when the cornstalks are dry as paper and the air smells of soot and ashes, Libby slides down off the split rail fence and starts walking. Before long, she finds herself in Alice's kitchen. Alice is slicing apples to bake a pie. She stands at the painted wooden table, a bowl in front of her, a paring knife in one hand, a pile of apples spread out on a tea towel.

"No school today?" Alice asks. She doesn't look up from her work.

Libby shakes her head. "Homecoming parade. I'm supposed to be working on a float."

Alice slices and slices. Libby looks out the window into the Prestons' yard where the wind whips up dust whirls and sighs through the trees. Alice lets her hands go limp in the bowl, puts her head back and closes her eyes.

"Where do they get all that tissue?" Alice says.

Libby's still standing by the door.

"I don't know. Trees, I guess."

"From Washington state?"

"Forest, you mean."

"Ocean, too. There's ocean there."

"San Francisco." Libby warms to this, now. "We could go to San Francisco."

"Walk across the Golden Gate Bridge." Alice smiles as she says this.

"You're afraid of heights, remember?"

"There's a railing."

"People fall off. People fall and they don't come back."

"Who's afraid now?"

Libby moves over to the cupboard. She opens a drawer and takes out a second paring knife.

"All right." Alice speaks softly to Libby. "We won't walk on the bridge."

Libby picks up an apple and begins to peel, one circular motion round and round. She does not look up from her work, and the peeling falls away in a long red spiral.

# BE CAREFUL WHAT YOU WISH FOR

BILLY, 1941

Billy hasn't had a bad life for a kid with no parents. Gramp and Grandma formally adopted him, wanting him to carry the Preston name. He had Nick and Timmy to play with until Mary married Richard Cuzak and moved a half mile down the road. Even then, the boys were back and forth often. Timmy drowned last year in Brown's Creek, a good swimmer but he dove in to save Haig Sugamo, and they were both sucked under by a whirlpool. Billy and some of the others managed to pull them out of the murky water and lay them out on the ditch bank. Nick stood over them while Billy ran for help, but no one was home at the first farmhouse, so he raced on to the McCoys, a full mile from the creek, and Mr. McCoy had then to drive into town.

Word got out and people, naturally curious, crowded the cow track with their trucks and cars so the rescue wagon couldn't get through. By the time the volunteers arrived, Haig was all but gone, so they put the one resuscitator the county could afford on him, and that mistake cost both boys their lives. Billy stood by helplessly, shifted his weight from foot to foot, gasped for breath as if he too were trapped beneath the water, and for months woke with recurring nightmares that left him wrung with fear and fatigue. He told no one. He hasn't spent more than fifteen minutes in Nick's company since, preferring to drive alone into the high school where he hugs the walls of the corridors and slips out before the last bell. He'd quit school if Gramp would allow it.

Gramp hardly speaks to him and never uses his name, calls him Old Kid and directs him to the chores. Grandma tries to make up for Gramp's sternness, for his mother's early dying, bakes him peach pie and turns down the handmade quilt on his bed at night. In her bib apron, her back hunched from a fall out of a wagon, thin white hair twisted into hairpins, she seems ancient to him, and fragile, like a prehistoric bird. She strokes his cheek, infuriating Gramp who says she'll make the boy soft and fit for nothing. They argue about him constantly, although they seldom speak. Instead, Gramp sits hunched in his rocking chair and aims foul tobacco juice toward a corner spittoon surrounded by newspaper, no longer caring if the cancer comes back. When Gramp slaps him, Grandma turns away and slips extra oatmeal cookies in his lunch. They live this way, an arced tension between them that exhausts him, but he is grateful for a roof over his head.

Today is Sunday, and Billy awakes feeling that this could be a good day. On winter Sundays Gramp and Grandma sit in morbid quiet, him reading and her sewing, and Billy takes to the fields. Today he rises before the sun, pulls on his clothes in a dark and chill room, slips his feet into socks and boots. He grabs a hunk of dark bread, slathers it with honey, closes the door quietly behind him so as not to wake them. He doesn't want Gramp calling him back.

By the time he's at the end of the lane, he's buttoned his coat, worked on his gloves, pulled down his hat and tied the flaps under his chin. He can see his breath and he plays at puffing out clouds of various size. On the horizon the sun crowns, while a sliver of white moon hangs ghostly in the western sky. He swings his arms and steps out with a long stride, the frozen earth crunching under his heels.

He takes his time, savoring dappled light on the gray tree limbs of a windbreak as the sun climbs up the sky. He hangs over the post of a barbed-wire fence and watches the morning cloaked in royal colors, pink and rose and gold, and thinks, not for the first time, that sunrise is when God tips his hand and lets the whole world know he's not the uptight bastard most assume him to be. Billy rotates his head to follow the circle of sky around him. He breathes deeply and stills himself to watch for deer or pheasants or grouse. His eyes trail a flock of ducks as they wave across the sky south toward the river where Russian olives and wild roses hug the banks and long prairie grass lies tangled in the hollows, protecting roots and seedlings that wait for the warmer days of spring.

He passes this way through several fields, walking down fallow rows of cornstalks that rustle against his pant legs, across pasture soggy with prairie dog hills and tufted with sage. Occasionally he stops to break pockets of ice and stoops to admire the crystals, the way the light turns them into prisms. He breaks off a dried milkweed and studies the shape of the pod, the lingering wisps of gauzy seed. His body is singing, he's young and there's room for him on this earth, space opening before him and behind him and around him as if to say enter here and you will find your way.

He travels this way for more than an hour and covers the three miles to Jake and Alice's place. He knows this has been his destination all along, but he has tricked himself into thinking of it as a surprise. They live now on this Henderson place, a rented basement house, yard rimmed by cottonwood trees, enough space for Alice to have a garden. Last summer after Stevie was born, Billy and Jake killed a big old rattlesnake that had settled onto the basement steps. They'd returned from a day in the fields and Alice was holed up inside the house, afraid to go out and climb the steps to daylight, her mood sour and frightened. She screamed at them as soon as she heard them step down from the truck, *snake, snake,* and Jake calmly picked up a hoe, hooked the snake and threw it onto the hard-packed dirt where Billy chopped at it with a shovel until certain it was dead. They left it lying where the dogs could get at it, and then Jake moved down the stairs and inside to comfort Alice. He'd held her, small against his broad chest, smoothed her curly flying hair with his hand, and Billy stood back watching, an ache in the back of his throat.

He's not sure what Jake is to him, more than uncle surely, not quite father. Together they shock acres of grain in a day, speechless and rhythmic, lifting sheaves in simultaneous arcs and bracing them upright with precise timing, their bodies humming like piano strings. They work side by side on Gramp's leased land, and Billy does what Jake tells him and Jake is his hero, and lately he's mad at him most of the time.

He raps now on the wooden screen door. It's Jake who comes to let him in, standing in a red plaid shirt and overalls, socks but no shoes. He's holding Stevie on his shoulder, the baby wrapped in cotton blankets, Jake's large hand patting him on the back. Jake says nothing, swings the door open and turns away. Billy moves on into the little kitchen where Alice stands over the cookstove stirring a skillet crammed with scrambled eggs. She's wearing a red robe knotted at the waist. The robe wraps around, and in the deep cut of the neckline, he can see a white nightgown underneath. Her hair is messy but beautiful, and her face shines like it has ever since she brought the baby home from the hospital.

"Just in time, Billy." Alice smiles but does not turn from the stove. He sees there are three places set at the table. Jake has already sat down and is dandling Stevie on his knee.

"Sure you don't mind?" Billy asks. He looks at Jake, but it's Alice who lifts her hand and gestures toward the table.

Billy unbuttons his coat and hangs it on a peg by the door. He sheds his boots, too, and then sits down at the table in his usual spot. When Alice sits, she puts her hand briefly on his shoulder, bracing herself, and where her hand touches him he feels a burning. He shrugs her hand off but wishes she'd leave it there a long time. Alice passes him a plate and he takes it from her, touching her hand and noticing the freckles sprayed across it, the chewed fingernails and her wedding ring. He studies her as she sits to the right of him, the tilt of her nose, her delicate ears. She has one small tooth that turns out slightly and she hates that about herself, but he likes it and is too shy to tell her. Mostly he likes knowing this about her, this one small imperfection and how she feels about it because he's sure she's never mentioned it to Jake.

"We got work to do today," Jake says, looking at Alice.

"What about church?"

"I need Billy's help getting those sugar beets out of the ground."

"I ain't digging those beets," Billy says.

Alice raises her eyebrows at him, and he shoots her a grin.

Jake takes a sip of coffee, doesn't raise his voice. "We don't get it done soon, it'll be Christmas. We got to get it done before the year's over."

"Then you can do it this afternoon," Alice says.

"Can't wait. Looks like snow this afternoon."

"We didn't make it to church last week."

"I'll take you into town, if you want. But you'll have to get a ride home with Gladys or somebody."

Alice stands and grabs Stevie out of Jake's arms. Startled, Stevie lets out a wail.

"Why'd you go and do that?" Jake says.

Alice has Stevie tucked against one hip, slinging plates around with her free arm.

"Because, if I got to go to church by myself, I got things to do."

Alice walks through the doorway into the living room and around the corner into the bedroom. Billy turns in his chair.

"You ain't the boss of me."

He's got one arm on the back of his chair, the other on the table, his chest lifted, his chin out. Jake picks up his coffee cup and drinks as if he's got all day. Billy sees Jake's hair nearly gone, the wire-rimmed glasses slipping down his nose, his teeth yellow and cobbled. He sees his big hands cradling the coffee cup, the same hands patting Stevie's back and smoothing Alice's hair. He wants to grab Jake's cup and smash it against the wall.

"You had no call to upset her like that. You know we ain't ever going to get those beets dug out whether we work on it today or a month of Sundays. The ground's froze. You're too damn stubborn to admit it."

"Gramp needs . . ."

"I don't care what Gramp needs. It ain't Gramp digging them."

"Maybe you'd like to go to church."

"Is that all this is about?"

"We got work to do."

"You got a wife."

Jake stops and looks at him. Billy notices the yellow blotches in the whites of Jake's eyes, same hazel eyes as Gramp's. He can't now and never could read what's going on inside Jake's head, but he won't look down. Not this time. Jake turns away, sets his coffee cup on the table, and speaks softly. "I sure do. I got a wife."

Later, after dropping Alice and Stevie in town, Billy having ridden between Alice and Jake, her arm flush against his, Stevie gurgling and double-chinned and grinning, Alice tight-lipped and frosty and her leg jiggling up and down against Billy's thigh, Alice not saying good-bye, slamming the door and jouncing into the First Baptist Church, waving her hand to Gladys and Marge and Jake watching until they're gone behind the doors, then driving back out to Gramp's, not even going up to the house, they get two shovels and two forks and then drive the truck down to the south field and get out and do not speak but put their shoulders to it. Billy sets the tines of the fork against the frozen ground and it's like attacking a mountain with a teaspoon. He puts his boot against the rim at the top of the fork and pushes with all his weight and barely breaks the surface. Jake already has his fork worked down under a fat sugar beet, patiently levering the huge clod of dirt that comes up with it, reaching down with gloved hand to break the earth and ice away and heave the freed sugar beet into the bed of the truck. He's on his second while Billy's still trying to get started, now jumping with both feet on the fork like it's a pogo stick. He knows he could break the fork, hopes he does, hopes Jake takes it to him, god, he thinks, this is a miserable day and the bright sun shines merciless down on them with glare and no heat.

Finally Billy gets his fork under a beet and levers it up and the ground is so solidly frozen that it heaves and buckles and his fork breaks free, spitting ice and chips of dirt and twanging against his hand and he's thrown back onto the ground. Jake keeps on edging his fork carefully and Billy can't stand this about the man, his silence and his plodding dutifulness, taking his time and doing it right, he's been years working this place for Gramp and what's it gotten him, and Alice deserves better than that basement house with rattlesnakes sunning on the only steps up out of the hole.

They have coffee in the truck and water, too, but Jake won't stop, not yet, not until their backs are breaking and their arms sore and their lips cracked from breathing the dry brittle air. Billy gets up and tries again, this time more successfully, the clump finally splitting off but the beet splitting with it, and he lets himself wonder what would happen if Jake got hurt. If he somehow stabbed himself with that fork. If he fell down on the earth and never got up, sun-stroke, winter-blinded, and Alice would need looking after.

They keep at this for a while, Jake methodically moving up the row and Billy battling every mound of dirt. Then Billy stands up and turns his face toward the west and realizes there's no snow. There's not going to be any snow, not today, and he's never known Jake to read the weather wrong.

"I ain't doing this." He says it in a low voice, one he's dredged up from someplace crusted over inside him.

"C'mon, we're making some headway now."

Billy bends and picks up a big clod of ice and frozen dirt and heaves it at Jake, narrowly missing his head and clipping him on the shoulder where he's stooped over the hard land. Jake turns, surprised. He stops and leans on the handle of the fork, looking at Billy with questions in his eyes and Billy nails him with another clod thrown fast and aimed in the middle of his chest.

"What the Sam Hill's the matter with you?"

Billy has his hand stretched reaching for another clump. He's working to break it free when Jake grabs him by the collar, lifts him like a mother cat carries her kittens, and shoves him up against the truck bed. Billy throws out his arms, pummels Jake's back, his arms, anywhere he can make contact and Jake puts his forearm across Billy's throat and holds him up against the bed of the truck. Jake's leaning on him, his whole body weight, Billy's hands clawing at his back, and Billy can taste the salty tears and then Jake lets him go. Just backs off and Billy slumps to the ground.

He runs then, takes off and once when he looks back, he sees Jake already bent over the rows, putting his muscles behind the fork, and Billy knows he'll be there until dark and he won't hardly make a dent in the field and the sugar beets will be lost anyway. He runs until his lungs hurt, he pushes himself gasping for air making sure they can't see him from the house skirting around the barn and the shed and following the windbreak across the pasture and nothing seems open to him now, the land rises up to crowd him, his feet trip over ditches, snarl in grass grabbing at his pant legs. By the time he reaches the Henderson place, he's a mess, snot running down his face, his cheeks blotchy, everything inside him about to blow up.

She's home and she's lit a kerosene lamp and from the above-ground window he looks in and watches her. She unbuttons her blouse, talking or maybe singing, her eyes dreamy and loving and looking at Stevie. She lets down the flap of her brassiere and her breast flowers, the nipple purple and swollen. He's hard between his legs and he puts his hand down and rubs himself while he watches Stevie take the nipple in his mouth and Alice rocks back and forth, back and forth, and he comes with a violent shudder and falls against the side of the house. He slumps there, his back against the stucco, his head thrown back eyes shut and tasting the salt and the grime and then, old as he is, he starts to cry.

After a while he cleans himself up. He wipes the snot off his face with his glove and then on his pants. He stands up and does not look through the window and moves away across the fields that seem foreign to him now. He walks where he is going blindly and fast, it's along toward dark and off across the pasture he sees Jake's truck heading home down the mile road.

When he walks in the back door of the house, he moves straight toward his room. He has one foot over the threshold when Gramp calls to him. He stops, braces his head on the doorjamb, does not turn around. What now? he asks himself. What the hell does that old man want now?

"Old Kid," Gramp calls again.

Billy turns and walks into the living room where Gramp sits in his rocking chair. The radio is on, maybe the batteries have run low and Gramp wants him to fire up the windcharger. Grandma is on the sofa, her hands folded in her lap, and that's his first clue that something is wrong.

"What is it? What's happened?"

He thinks of Jake driving home. An accident, surely. How could they have heard so quickly? The horror rises in his throat and though he knows he didn't mean it when he wished him dead, he's thinking this is his fault and isn't this just his luck to get a wish the one time he truly doesn't want it.

"Old Kid, the Japs bombed Pearl Harbor today."

"Oh," Billy says, relief leaving him weak in the knees. He falls down into the nearest chair.

Gramp misreads him. "Don't worry. Farmers will be needed at home."

Billy only looks at Gramp blankly. He stands then and moves stiffly toward his room to lie down. He lies in the dark and tries to picture the world of his future, but he doesn't get very far, not even past the front lane and the mailbox. He turns on his narrow cot, his back against the wall and his face toward the shadows in the room, and because he is young and his body aching and exhausted, he sleeps.

# ELITCH GARDENS

ALICE, 1942

Alice is twenty-two, the only one who's married and a mother, and yet she's the smallest of the three sisters. She weighs ninety-nine pounds, and in a swingy skirt and platform shoes she pirouettes like a kid. Grace stands the same height as Alice, but she's rounder, has short, mousy hair and looks tired all the time. She lives alone in an apartment in Denver and wears sensible shoes and rides a bus five days a week to a mechanics' shop where she works as a secretary. Libby's the youngest and full figured, like Betty Grable, a doll, and the reason she could ride the train with Alice to visit Grace in Denver is because she's on summer leave from her teaching job up by Hemingford.

The three of them are crowded into Grace's kitchen,

the window open and yet the air stifling. A wad of paper under one short leg keeps the second-hand table from wobbling. Stevie, who's almost a year old now, sits tied to a chair with a dish towel, peas dribbling down his chin. He's wearing short yellow pants and a white shirt with embroidered ducks. Grace bustles around, dishing up fried chicken, mashed potatoes.

"Sit down, Grace. You're wearing me out." Alice rolls her eyes at Libby, and Libby smiles.

"I've got pie for dessert." Grace thumps down in her chair.

"You must have gotten up early to get that done. Didn't you have church today?"

"What kind of pie?" Libby asks.

"Cherry." Then, raising her chin at Alice. "I baked it before church."

"I always loved your pie, Grace. Momma said you make the best pie."

Grace beams at Libby's praise. "The two of you were too young to bake a pie before Momma died."

A slight pall descends on the little trio. Alice's hand freezes mid-air with a spoon full of mashed potatoes aimed toward Stevie's open mouth. Libby's fingers stop plucking at the wayward hair that won't stay behind her ears. Grace looks down at her lap.

"C'mon," Alice says. "This is my vacation. If I wanted this sour mood, I could've stayed home with Jake."

"What's wrong with Jake?" Grace asks.

"Oh, nothing really. The fields are too wet. Or else, it doesn't rain. I'm so sick of farming; I don't care if I never see another ear of corn."

Grace stands and stacks plates at the table. "You two girls can have my bed. I'll sleep on the couch."

"I'll take the couch."

"Let me. I'm the youngest."

"I know you two will want to be together."

"Grace, don't be like that," Alice snaps.

"Besides, you say I snore."

"You do snore."

"Well, I can't help that."

"Let's all three sleep in the bed, like we used to," Libby offers, always the peacemaker.

"I'd still snore."

"We don't mind. Do we Alice?"

"We'll just roll you over."

"There won't be much room for rolling."

"What about Stevie?"

"He can sleep on a blanket on the floor."

"We'll have to pen him in."

"I've got that old trunk and a chair we can use."

"All right. That's settled, then."

They clear the table of the supper dishes, slice cherry pie, pour three cups of coffee and sit down again.

"What will you two girls do while I'm at work?"

"Maybe we'll sleep 'til noon." Alice sweeps her arms wide and hugs herself. "No chores. No dogs to feed. No men folk to cook for."

"Won't Stevie be up?" Grace asks.

"Stevie's no trouble," Libby says. "Besides, we don't want to waste our holiday sleeping. I want to go to the shops."

"I can't spend any money."

"We can look, can't we?"

"I want to go to the movies."

"That costs money," Grace says.

"For gosh sakes, Grace. Why did you invite us if you don't want us to have any fun?" Alice rescues a cherry-laden spoon from Stevie's grasp.

"You said you couldn't spend money."

"How much?" Libby asks.

"I bet it's not that much," Alice says.

"Forty cents for adults," Grace warns. Then, as if offering a concession, "Stevie can get in for free."

"How much for kids?" Alice asks.

"Twenty-five, but you and Libby aren't kids."

Alice steals a look at Libby, and Libby smiles. That quickly they fall back into the girls they used to be. Without speaking, Alice and Libby have a plan, and they won't bother to tell Grace. And that's just the way it goes.

The next three mornings Grace trudges off to work after making them all coffee and pancakes or French toast or eggs and bacon. She insists and complains and they help her clean up and then she's gone. Alice and Libby dress Stevie and go out and walk the streets and look in shop windows and try on dresses they could never afford, short jackets with shoulder pads, slim skirts to save fabric for the war effort, and when they emerge in their print dresses with accent buttons down the front and puffy sleeves, they feel outdated and wasteful and unpatriotic. Stevie's a jewel, hardly ever squawks, and sometimes Alice stops to breast feed him in a dressing room, although for the most part he's done with that. They take him home late in the morning so he can have a short nap. They eat a light lunch, something they've bought cheap at a sandwich shop or they just see what falls out of Grace's refrigerator, a luxury Alice can't believe. Grace has indoor plumbing, too, and while Libby coaxes her hair into a roll high above her forehead the way they've seen on the store mannequins, Alice takes a second bath, not caring that the steam makes her hair even curlier and impossible to coax.

In the afternoon they go to a matinee at the Mayan, a different film every day for three days featuring Clark Gable. It's the saddest thing, the way Carole Lombard died in that plane crash in January, and everybody knows Clark can't pull himself together and that's why he's enlisted in the Army Air Corps. The newsreels are full of shots of him moving through his new life as a soldier, and then the old movies where he looks like a young insolent god, that scene in *It Happened One Night* where he takes his shirt off and Libby and Alice can't get enough of him.

This is the way they manage it. When they are a block away from the movie theater, Libby saddles Stevie against one hip. Alice walks in slightly ahead of them and buys a child's ticket. No one ever questions her. Libby buys an adult ticket, and they splurge and share popcorn. The newsreels make them feel sad for the boys overseas and scared for their brother Edward who's off training in radio school and especially sorry for poor Clark whose life has fallen apart and now he's doing the brave and noble thing. They laugh through the cartoons and weep when Claudette Colbert or Jeanette McDonald falls into Clark's arms at last.

They're back home before Grace gets there, and as soon as they've had a bite to eat, they're on the go again, walking the streets at night, Alice and Libby dazzled by the neon signs and street lights and all the people, and once they go into Woolworth's which is open in the evening and sit at a counter and order coffee and pie.

They go on this way for three days, running every minute. Grace grows more and more tired with all the staying up late, but Alice and Libby feel liberated and less like themselves with every passing day which is how they end up at Elitch Gardens on Thursday and why they let those men tag along.

They notice the boys watching them in front of the carousel. They look young, eighteen or nineteen, closer to Libby's age, both of them dressed in town clothes, pressed trousers and clean plaid shirts. The taller one has blond hair that droops over his eyes, almost like Clark's. The shorter one's dark hair is cropped above his ears, a cowlick giving him a rooster tail that Libby thinks is funny, but Alice says it's kind of sweet, and they smile at the boys.

They move on from the carousel to the fun house. Stevie laughs and tries to grab at the elongated baby in the mirror, and Alice makes it through the rolling barrels without losing either her balance or her grip on Stevie. She and Libby take turns on the spinning floor, sitting near the center until they are flung to the outside edge, skirts flying, and they leave the fun house laughing and slightly nauseous and drooping.

The boys are waiting for them outside the door. Alice and Libby smile and the four of them move off together as if they are old friends.

"What are you girls going to try next?" The tall blond one says this, looking at Libby.

"Can we take you on the Ferris wheel?" The shorter one blurts this out like he's been rehearsing it, and he says it to Alice's shoes.

"Wait a minute. We don't even know you boys' names," Libby says.

The tall one takes over. "I'm John, and he's Clint."

"I'm Libby."

"I'm Alice."

"Whose baby is that?" John asks.

Alice looks at Libby, and Libby says, "Our sister's. We're watching him while she's at work."

"Oh, well. That's okay then."

Alice says nothing to correct Libby, her mind on what she's supposed to do about her wedding ring. She reaches into the bag she carries for Stevie and pulls out a clean cloth diaper. She pretends to mop Stevie's face with it and then keeps it in her hand, careful to drape the fabric over her ring. "He spits up all the time," she says. "You never know when it might happen."

"You girls had lunch yet?" John asks.

"Maybe not," Alice says.

"How about if we treat you to a hamburger over in the pavilion?" John asks.

"Then we can go on the Ferris wheel," Clint adds, risking a grin in Alice's direction.

Libby looks at Alice and raises her eyebrows. Alice shrugs and laughs. "Okay, I guess."

They find a table in the noisy pavilion and the boys go up to the counter to order for them. Libby and Alice slip off to the women's restroom where they crowd into one stall.

"Why'd you go and tell them Stevie's not mine?"

"I don't know. It just came out."

"What if he starts calling me momma?"

"He calls every woman momma."

"They don't know that."

"We'll tell them."

"What about my wedding ring?"

"Take it off."

"I can't take it off."

"Why not?"

"Because, I can't. What would I do with it?"

"Put it in your brassiere."

"What if I have to nurse Stevie? I might forget and lose it."

"Give it to me. I'll put it in my brassiere."

"I could put it in my shoe."

"Be careful or you'll drop it in the toilet."

They start laughing then, bumping into each other while they take turns peeing, passing Stevie back and forth who all this time grins goofily up into the face of whoever holds him.

"Libby, what are we doing?"

"Getting free hamburgers."

They sit with the boys through lunch and eat hamburgers and French fries and drink Coca-cola. The boys are cousins. John is from Cheyenne and Clint from a ranch near Laramie, and they've met up here while they are waiting for the train that will take them to San Diego and basic training. They're nice boys and they act brave and because Libby and Alice feel sorry for them and are thinking about Clark Gable, they agree to ride the Ferris wheel with them.

John sits with Libby in one tilting chair and Clint rides with Alice and Stevie. When they go up over the top and Alice's stomach slides, she notices that in the chair ahead John moves his arm around Libby. Clint sits shy and polite beside Alice.

"Your momma must be sad about you leaving," Alice says.

Clint shrugs. "I guess so."

"You got a sweetheart at home?"

"Sort of."

"What's her name?"

"Dorothy. We went to the prom together. I don't know if she'll wait for me."

"She will if she loves you."

"I don't know if she loves me."

The motion of the Ferris wheel puts Stevie to sleep and he lies draped heavily over Alice's arm.

"Here. Let me take him."

"Oh no, that's all right," but Clint has already reached out and taken Stevie and tucked him into the crook of his elbow.

"You look like you've had practice at that."

"Yeah. I got little brothers and sisters."

"How many?"

"Nine."

"Oh, my goodness."

They ride quietly, looking out over the amusement park crowded with families. It's hard to think there's a war going on while looking down on children with balloons and people pink-mouthed with smeared cotton candy.

When the ride is over, Clint shifts Stevie to his shoulder. They meet up with Libby and John who are holding hands, and Alice starts to worry about where this is headed.

"Libby, we better be going home," Alice says.

"We'll see you home," John says, his gaze dreamy and fixed on Libby.

"You can walk us to the bus stop," Libby says.

"We'll ride the bus with you," John says.

"Oh, you." Libby laughs and shoves against him with her hip.

Alice raises her eyebrows at Libby, wondering if she has any idea how they'll get rid of the boys once they get to Grace's apartment.

At the bus stop Alice stares at a poster of a farmer in overalls, a pitchfork in his hand, Stay Home and Serve in bold red and blue. When the bus comes, they file on and pair off. Alice studies the diagram of the stops. Two stops before the one closest to Grace's apartment, she tugs the bell rope. Reaching to take Stevie from Clint, she smiles, and to Libby who is sitting one seat ahead and not paying attention, she says, "This is us, Libby."

John gets up to follow Libby and motions to Clint, and the boys step off the bus at the same stop. Alice crowds John out so she can walk by Libby. Clint lags behind. At the first apartment building, Alice grabs Libby by the arm. "Well, here we are." She glares a warning at Libby to play along. Libby smiles, and Alice hauls her up the walk into the strange apartment building, calling out good-bye to Clint over her shoulder, and when she gets Libby in the foyer, she's furious.

"What are you doing? We can't let those boys know where we're staying. What would Grace have to say about that?"

Alice watches out the corridor window to make sure the boys move down the street before she and Libby step out to walk the remaining eight blocks to Grace's apartment.

"Oh, Alice. You worry too much."

"Somebody has to."

"You could hurt their feelings."

"We'll never see them again."

Libby says nothing until they reach Grace's building. Then, while they climb the stairs to the third floor, she quietly confesses. "I told John we'd meet them at the Rainbow Ballroom tonight."

"You what?"

"Jimmie James's band is playing."

"We're not going."

"What can it hurt?"

"And what are we going to tell Grace?"

"Nothing. She can come, too. She doesn't have to know anything."

"What about Stevie?"

"That's never stopped you before."

Outside Grace's apartment door Alice puts a hand on Libby's elbow and turns her so they are face to face. "Are you falling for this boy?"

Libby shrugs. "It's their last night. Their train leaves at four in the morning. And they don't know anybody else."

It turns out that Grace has a headache and has already decided to turn in early. She's too tired to care what Alice and Libby are up to. Alice promises nothing all the while she's putting Stevie to bed. Once he's asleep and Grace snoring softly, Libby heads for the bathroom and gets out her lipstick. Alice stands in the doorway, leaned against the jamb, arms crossed in front of her. She watches Libby's face in the mirror.

"You're too young to be this old," Libby says. She turns and offers her lipstick, the look on her face clearly a dare.

Alice takes the lipstick, steps up to the mirror and paints her mouth red. She pinches her cheeks and turns to check her silhouette. Tossing her head at Libby, she says, "I think I'll wear my green dress."

The girls show up looking ripe for a party. Alice has tied a green ribbon in her hair, the bow on top of her head. She looks even younger, but festive. Her green dress has a wide white collar with black buttons on the corners. Libby has achieved the perfect jelly-rolled hairdo, and she shimmers in a light gray dress with a black belt and black embroidered stitching around a square neckline.

John and Clint swoop down on the girls, and John leads Libby out on to the dance floor.

"Want to give it a try?" Clint asks.

"I don't know how," Alice says, but she goes with him and lets him put his arm around her and slips her hand in his. They move back and forth on the edge of the crowd. When the music gets fast, Clint and Alice step outside onto a small wooden deck. Above them the slivered moon hangs by a corner.

"I leave in the morning." Clint leans his elbows on the railing.

"I know. Libby told me." Alice smiles at Clint.

"There's a guy from Laramie who got shot in basic training. They brought him home in a box. He didn't even make it to the war."

"You'll be all right."

"People've been real kind to me. Some volunteers came to the Oxford yesterday and left packages of homemade cookies for all the troops. I got sugar cookies. Not as good as my mom's, but close enough."

"That's nice."

"So I feel pretty lucky."

They stand a while in silence. Alice's arm brushes Clint's as she leans against the railing. She feels a heat rising in her, and she's ashamed of it, but she doesn't move her arm.

"Will you write to me?"

"Oh, Clint. I . . . I got something to tell you."

"Stevie's yours, isn't he?"

Alice nods her head. "I left my wedding ring home in the dresser."

"Okay. I see how it is."

"Don't get mad. It's just, Libby, well, we wanted some fun, and you boys were alone, and I guess I should have told you before."

"That's all right."

"You're a real nice boy, Clint."

"How come your husband isn't in the war?"

"He's a farmer."

"Then he's doing his part."

"Like that poster, you mean?"

"Sure. Somebody's got to grow food for the troops."

"Why aren't you staying on your father's ranch?"

Clint ducks his head. "Well, there's a lot of us. I've got brothers to help Dad."

Alice looks away. She raises a finger to her lips and bites her nail. "I hate farming. It's just a lot of hard work and still we're dirt poor."

"Safe, though," Clint offers.

Alice turns and grabs Clint's sleeve. She's trembling, and he puts his hand over hers.

"Whoa. What's the matter?"

"Oh Clint, I get so frightened sometimes. For you. For all our boys."

"Sh-h-h. Don't talk like that. It will all be over soon."

She lets him turn her back to the railing. They rest against it, but he hasn't let go of her hand. She notices the dark hair on Clint's arm, compares the size of his wrist to hers. Her breathing is jumpy and something in her chest hurts.

"What are you doing here?" he asks.

"Libby and I are visiting our sister. That part's true."

"You must have got married real young."

"Seventeen. Jake's older than me, some."

Clint turns and puts his hand under Alice's chin, raising her face to his. "When John and I saw the two of you, I said I want that little one. I picked you out straight away. And I'm not sorry that I got to know you, Alice."

"I'm not sorry either, Clint."

"Would you mind if . . . ? I mean . . ."

Alice touches her hand to Clint's cheek and nods. "You can pretend I'm Dorothy if you want to."

"No. That's not what I want."

He touches his lips to hers and Alice lets him hold her close to his chest and she gives herself to the kiss, to this boy who's going to a foreign country to come back forever changed or not come back at all. She puts her hands behind his head, and the kiss is long and deep.

After that they dance slow together and Alice lets Clint drink her in with his eyes. He squeezes her hand, and she squeezes back, and when they leave, she rests her head against Clint's shoulder on the bus ride.

"Didn't we go past your sister's stop?" Clint asks. Alice smiles and makes an apologetic face, and he nods with understanding. They ride on until the stop in front of Grace's apartment. The two boys walk them to the door, and John and Libby linger kissing in the shadows while Alice stands with Clint under the glare of the outside bulb.

"Don't forget me, Alice," Clint says.

"No, I won't. I won't ever forget," she says.

Clint grabs for her hand, and Alice shrinks back, wanting to lift his fingers to her cheek. She sees the hurt on his face, and without considering how it will pain her to keep him in her thoughts, she says, "I'll pray for you. Would you like that?"

"I guess I would."

Finally they part, and on the way up the stairs, Alice asks Libby. "Did you tell John the truth?"

"No. Did you?"

"Didn't he say anything about coming to a different apartment?"

"I don't think he noticed." Libby rolls her eyes at Alice and laughs.

"Did you promise to write?"

"No. He didn't even ask for my address. I bet he's got a girlfriend somewhere."

Three more steps, and then Alice asks. "Do you mind?"

Libby stops and her face holds surprise, like she's just turned the crank on a jack-in-the-box. "I guess I do."

Alice puts her arms around her sister and they stand together in the corridor outside Grace's apartment and weep. When they finish, they dry their eyes and slip into the apartment, and while Libby uses the bathroom, Alice picks Stevie up from his bed on the floor and holds the sleeping boy to her bosom and rocks back and forth in the spilling moonlight.

# NEVER MIND

MARY, 1944

Mary straightens Nick's collar while they wait at the train station in Elmyra. She smoothes the lapels of his coat, then licks her fingers and tames down a tuft of hair that shoots up. He looks about twelve to her, not nearly old enough to join a war.

"Ma, would you cut it out?" Nick grabs his mother's hand as it wanders toward his shoulders. Mary whacks him on the arm. She has to touch him. "Ma," Nick says again, as she fiddles with his cuffs.

Mary glances around at other young men and parents and sweethearts, all waiting for the midnight train to Denver. From there Nick will board another train to San Diego where he'll finish his navy schooling and ship out.

Mary has never ridden a train in her life. The moment Nick steps aboard that metal beast, he'll be a long ways away from her.

A couple moves from one of three benches that face the tracks, and Nick offers his mother a seat. She shakes her head. She can't sit still. She watches the couple move outside to find a corner of privacy, hears the clop of their shoes on the brick platform. She clutches her handbag in both hands, squeezing so hard her hands ache. There are things she wants to tell Nick. Warnings. Cocky young men die, she knows this for a fact. She's lost two husbands. And didn't Nick's older brother Timmy drown in Pumpkin Creek because he tried to save Haig Sugamo? These are strange times we're living in, she wants to say, look what happened to Haig's family, rousted out to that camp in Montana. So beware. Don't try to be a hero. And come home.

Instead, she stands in silence and grips her bag. She watches Nick to memorize his quick grin, the way he stands with one hand on the back of his neck. He has dark eyes like his father's, a teasing Greek man whose memory still makes Mary's blood run warm.

In the corner of the depot a small child cries and clings to the legs of a young man Mary doesn't recognize. A slender woman scoops up the child and cradles her against a soft shoulder. Mary turns away and sets her eyes on the gum-dispensing machine, Chiclets in miniature boxes, a positive return for every nickel.

"I still wish I could have helped you move."

"You have helped. You've been putting Ruth and Helen's things in boxes for weeks. Every time they want something to wear, they have to go through another box."

The train lumbers into the station, snorting and bellowing smoke that drifts wide across the prairie. People pour out onto the platform, young men spilling into the cars, the crowd strangely silent. To one side a woman weeps, but no one looks at her.

Nick turns, finally, to Mary and throws his arms around her.

She brushes her cheek against the rough wool of his coat and presses one hand flat against his back, the other still clutching her handbag. When she leans back to study his face, she detects a flicker of uncertainty. She sees in an instant what he needs from her, and so she gives it to him.

"Go on, Nick. Your train's leaving."

Nick raises her fingers to his lips, his eyes watching her over their linked hands. It's a silly, romantic gesture, something he must have seen in the movies, but she laughs gaily, and when his back is turned and he moves away from her, she clasps her hands together and gathers the warmth of his lips, and it's enough to get her through watching the train pull away from the platform.

Days later, Mary stands shivering in her new front yard, a space smaller than her old chicken pen. She's huddled in a tattered brown corduroy coat, holding the ends of a triangular-folded wool scarf. She doesn't bother to tie the scarf because she's just stepped out to get some air. To get away from her girls. They squabble constantly, but Mary doesn't have the energy to do much about it.

Far cry from the farm, she says out loud. Mary and others like her, women or men too old for the war with no place else to go, have been hired to work at the Sioux Ordnance Depot, a munitions plant ten miles west of Sidney. They live here, in Ordville, at a subsidized rate. The officers live in houses across the road where's there's a cafeteria, a school, and a little base store. Big warehouses hold the office management workers, where Mary will show up every day to count and tally receipts, but most of the men and some of the women work in concrete bunkers that stretch for miles, rows and rows of inverted grass-covered cones. Not a tree in sight.

Mary looks at the tiny side-by-side yards, the rows of one-story stucco units. Some yards are lined with white picket fences. She can't see the point of that. Nobody wants to be here that long.

She looks to the west and follows the line of the horizon and wonders if the same sky will settle over Nick. She knows the stars will be different in his part of the world.

Two doors down, Mary's neighbor steps out onto her front stoop. She has carrot red hair, and she's come out to smoke a cigarette. Mary disapproves of smoking, especially for women. She disapproves of hair that color, too. The woman turns to look at her, and Mary can see that she has a black eye. The bruise spreads down one side of her face, ugly and blotched, and the woman does not turn away but stares right at her. God almighty. What will become of her girls living in a place like this?

On Monday Mary sits in a room full of thirty women listening to Mr. Grenby explain how they are to fill out forms and file them in alphabetical order. He lists the forms on the blackboard and impresses upon them that each form has to be filled out for each different shipment of ammunition. Otherwise the army won't know where its weapons are and boys will die far from home. He says this over and over. If they don't do their jobs right, boys will die far from home.

Mary sits quietly, as do all the other women, but then the room starts to stir. The women shuffle their feet and clear their throats. The man appears not to notice and goes on listing and counting and naming forms and warning them.

"Excuse me." From the back of the room. Mary turns and sees her red-haired neighbor standing up, waving one hand in the air. Her dress is a screaming shade of chartreuse, her lips painted bright red, her ears pierced and jangling with gold hoops.

Everyone turns to look at her. Mr. Grenby adjusts his glasses on his nose and recovers enough to glower. "Yes?"

"Stop saying that. How do you expect us to work if you go on saying that our boys will die if we don't put the right number on a piece of paper? We are not the enemy here."

"Ma'am, if you would sit down." Mr. Grenby stands taller and puffs out his chest. He's not that old, thirty maybe, with thick glasses and a schoolboy air about him. He wears a brown uniform with some stripes on his sleeve, but Mary has no idea what they mean.

"My boy's over there," a woman in the third row states. "I'm working here to help the war effort."

"Ladies, please, if you would settle down."

"Mr. Grenby," the red-haired woman says. "Why aren't you fighting in the war?"

A few of the younger women snicker. A blonde in a black-ribbed sweater says, "What's the matter with you? Flat feet?"

Then, a quiet dignified woman rises. She's a sturdy young woman who speaks simply. "My husband died at Midway." The room falls hushed. Mary watches as one woman after another rises to her feet. One by one the women name their loved ones who have died, a brother in France, a nephew at Guadalcanal, a fiancé from encephalitis before he even shipped out, until seven women are standing, six in mourning and the red-haired woman who refuses to sit down. In two and threes the others begin to stand, and while Mary is not the first to gain her feet, she is not the last, and soon the whole room full of silent women faces Mr. Grenby who cowers against the blackboard with his hands braced behind him. Trembling, he manages to bring his hands out from behind his back. He removes his glasses and wipes them on the sleeve of his shirt. He takes a long time doing it. Then, he looks out but not at them, his gaze placed distinctly into the space above their heads. "Tomorrow." His voice squeaks, and he tries again. "We'll resume this tomorrow."

Six weeks later Mary stands outside after dark with the red-haired woman whose name is Irene. It's December and cold, but Irene doesn't smoke in the house. They've taken to this habit of meeting after their kids are in bed, before Irene's no-good husband makes his way home from Ollie's Bar. Mary folds her arms around her body while Irene leans up against the side of the house and blows smoke at the stars.

"There's the Big Dipper," Irene says.

"Little Dipper, too."

"Where?"

"Follow those two stars on the end of the Big Dipper. See? That star's the tail end of the Little Dipper, the North Star."

"I didn't know that."

"Shoot, Irene. Who raised you, anyway?"

"Nobody. I told you that."

The two women laugh, low and throaty.

"Heard from Nick?" Irene asks this every night.

"Yesterday, I told you. He's still floating in the Pacific."

"He'll be all right."

Mary nods silently, not wanting to jinx Nick's chances by claiming too much. Irene starts coughing and leans forward with her hand braced against the house.

"There goes Buzz," Mary says. They watch as Buzz Simmons comes out of Marla Jenner's house and walks past them in the lane.

"Evenin', Buzz," Irene calls.

Buzz doesn't look up at them.

After he's moved on by, Mary speaks. "Why do you do that?"

"Do what?"

"Embarrass him like that?"

"Oh, I don't know. Maybe it gives me a little comfort to laugh at human nature once in a while."

"I don't find human nature very funny."

"Don't you?"

"No. I don't. I think it's sorrowful most of the time."

"Yeah, that's true."

"So what's funny about that?"

"Well." Irene takes her time, dumping ash off the end of her cigarette into the dirt yard. "I guess either we're laughing or the joke's on us."

Mary tightens the scarf under her chin. "It's too cold to be out here."

"C'mon, stick it out a while." Irene laces her arm through Mary's and draws her closer. Mary's round hip bumps up against Irene's bony thigh. "Tell me something funny."

"I don't know anything funny."

"C'mon."

They are silent for a while, Irene blowing smoke from her cigarette and Mary searching the sky for Orion and wishing on every other star for Nick's safe return.

"I thought of something," Mary says.

"Good girl. I'm all ears."

"I told you how Pop is, how he has that spittoon in the corner of the living room and how he won't pay taxes on any land. After Chris died—"

"Your first husband?"

"Yeah. After Chris died, I hid the money from the sale in a sock."

"What sale?"

"He had a few acres. Pop thought we best sell since I couldn't work it."

"Okay. Go on."

"I hid the money in a sock for a while, and then I put it in the bank. I thought it was safer."

Mary pauses. "Seems right," Irene says, to prod her along.

"It was 1929," Mary says.

"Jesus."

"Pop came flying home from town one day. Said he heard something at Cooper's Feed and Seed and we better get to town in a hurry. I was hanging clothes on the line, my mouth rimmed with clothespins, and he hollered, *leave 'em be*, and I jumped in the truck. He hit every rut in the road. I thought sure we'd be shook to pieces or off in the ditch. We got to the bank, but it was too late. The door was locked with a sign posted on it. Closed. Like that. All that money gone."

Mary is laughing now, her eyes filling with tears, her breath locked inside her and making her gasp. "You know what Pop said?"

Irene turns to her. "What'd he say?"

"He hitched at the straps of his overalls, looked right into the glare of the sun, and then he said, Never mind."

"Never mind?" Irene echoes, her own voice rising. "Never mind?"

Mary makes her voice low and quiet, firm like her father's. "Never mind."

The two of them dissolve in laughter. They lean against each other for support, their legs buckling. They laugh until they run down and their fingers are numb and then they whisper good night and Mary turns to her door and Irene disappears behind hers.

One night in January, in the wee hours of the morning, Mary wakes to a knock on her door. She closes the girls' bedroom door and crosses her tiny living room and kitchen. She moves the curtain aside to look out and sees Irene huddled against the door in her nightgown. It's torn down one side, and she's barefoot.

Mary throws her door open. Irene hides her face from her, but Mary can see she's in trouble. She grabs an old blanket off the couch and throws it around Irene's shoulders. Blood from Irene's nose drips onto Mary's floor. Mary sits her down at the kitchen table, runs the tap and soaks a dish towel that she wads up and presses against Irene's face.

"Thanks," Irene murmurs, and Mary turns to put on the teakettle.

"Don't say anything," Irene says.

Mary locks her lips tightly together. This isn't the first time Irene's shown up at her door. They got to be friends in the first place because Irene had landed here, like this, not two weeks after Mary moved in. That time the sonofabitch locked her out.

"He'll pass out pretty soon. Then I can go back."

"Irene—" but Mary stops at Irene's uplifted hand.

Irene cleans herself up and draws the blanket close around her while Mary busies herself with the tea, dropping one bag into a cup, filling it with water, moving the same bag to the second cup. She puts a pinch of sugar into each steaming cup. Then she sits down across from Irene and surveys the damage. A fat lip and a bloody nose, a cheek starting to swell. No cuts or bruises on her arms. No bald patches where he yanked her hair. This isn't the worst time, then.

"Are the boys all right?"

"Yeah, I think so. They were asleep when he came in. He won't hurt them."

Mary looks away. She's seen Irene's two boys with scabs on their arms and bruises. The little one, Mickey, has developed a facial tic.

They drink their tea in silence. Irene sniffles at first, but eventually she quiets. She rubs her own shoulders and the back of her neck.

"Mary, do you think these are the best years of our lives?"

Mary thinks for a minute that Irene has gone completely crazy.

She studies her for signs, but can't see anything that unusual. "I hope not," she says and attempts a laugh.

"Think about it. We're young. Well, fairly young. We still have all our teeth."

They chuckle together.

"And we get a paycheck. Don't tell me you don't like that."

"Sure, I like it, Irene, but what's that got to do with anything?"

"Right now, I could make my own way if I could get Herb to leave."

"You should. You should make him move out."

"I know, but Mary," and now Irene leans forward and starts to whisper. "They're saying the war could be over soon. And you know what that means?"

"Sure. Nick will come home. Safe."

"Nick and all the other men. And they'll need jobs. And then what's going to happen to us?"

Mary gathers her robe closer. She's been holding her breath until Nick gets home safely. Nick and Edward and all the other boys. She knows women who light candles every day.

"Don't talk like that," Mary says, standing and moving away from the table.

"You know they only hired women because they had to."

"I don't want to hear that."

A pause stretches between them. Irene softens her voice. "Why don't you sit down? You're making me nervous."

Mary sits and picks up her tea cup and brings the hot liquid to her lips. She tries to think of something to say, but she's all clogged up. Why's Irene got to go and bring up notions like that? She can't think like that, it would make her crazy. Besides, she's been counting the days until she can get her girls out of this hellhole. This is no kind of home. This life isn't even real, it's a package the government dreamed up to get its dirty work done. After the war, things will be better. No rationing. No worry. After the war, Nick will be home, and she'll find something better for her girls. She'll get a job in a bank, maybe. Why not? If she can count bombs, she can count money.

"You're wrong, Irene. Things are going to get better."

Irene leans her head back, holding a bloody tissue to her nose. "It's just going to be different. That's all."

Mary watches her own hands tumble over themselves in her lap. "Things are always different," she says, making Irene laugh.

On a blustery day in March, Mary helps Irene load the last of her things into a broken down Ford. The two boys are in the back seat, their feet perched high on boxes and suitcases. Helen and Ruth keep knocking on the windows, and the boys pretend not to notice but roll the windows up and down, egging the girls on.

Finally, Mary stands with Irene at the hood of the car. The wind whips across the open plain and flips their skirts, but they don't bother to hold them down. They let the wind have its way, for once, and the air is warm, so what does it matter?

"Write to me," Mary says.

"Course," Irene promises, but Mary knows she won't. Writing's hard for Irene, and that's why they've let her go from her job. She covered it up for a long while with her humor and bravado, getting other people to do the writing for her, she's quick enough and memorizes easily, and nobody would have known if Buzz Simmons's wife hadn't ratted on her.

"One good thing, you got rid of Herb."

"Yeah," Irene says, but she turns away. Herb's staying here, shacked up with some young girl in a trailer parked north of town.

"How long a drive is it?"

"Oh, couple of days. I got an old friend we can stay with in Chadron. I'm just going back home to South Dakota 'til I can get my feet on the ground."

"I know."

"My sister, Josie, she's good to me and all. Her husband's got a good job. He's too old for the war."

Mary nods. They've been over this, but they're trying to stretch the time between them.

"Well." Irene throws her arms around Mary. "Nick'll be home soon." She whispers this in Mary's ear. "I know it. And you know how I am when I know something."

She loosens herself and walks straight to her car. She gives Helen and Ruth each a hug, gets in, starts the motor and backs away. At the end of the alley, she toots the horn and waves, and then she's gone.

Mary stands in the alley for a while, watching the dust settle and how the light glints off it. She raises her head to the west and stretches her eyes out along the horizon to a distant clump of cottonwoods and back again.

The girls have gone to the house ahead of her. When she comes in, they are sitting on the couch, their hands quiet in their laps. Mary worries about them constantly, growing up in this place, without a father, two girls. What's to become of them?

She turns to put on the teakettle and sits down at the kitchen table. The girls have not moved and she cannot bring herself to go to them the way she knows she should. When the water starts to boil, Mary rises and pours water over a tea bag into a cup. She pours two more cups of water using the same teabag. She rations sugar into each cup and sets all three on the table.

"Girls, what do you say we build a picket fence around our front yard?"

Ruth looks at Helen and shrugs. Helen turns her face toward her mother's.

"With flowers?"

"Lots of flowers."

"Red ones?" Ruth asks.

"Why not?"

The girls laugh and jump up like colts let out to pasture. Mary watches until they quiet and join her at the table, and there they are, the three of them, planning for the future while the March wind blows across the open prairie.

# GOOD-BYE, OLD KID

BILLY, 1945

Thursday morning and Billy stands out in the tool shed cleaning his rifle. It's April, too early for planting. He's been putting in long hours, keeping things shipshape while Jake visits Alice at the hospital and takes care of Stevie. He's got plans to drive down to Bickford later to see Hattie, the unmarried sister of the girl he once loved. He tried for Noreen, but she married Roscoe, and Hattie's not half bad.

He hears Jake's truck pull into the yard. Jake's come to see Gramp who's taken to his bed after a stroke. He's been in that bed almost two weeks, and no one knows whether he's going to get up again.

"Don't forget to sharpen up those disk blades," Jake says, sticking his head around the corner of the shed. Stevie makes a flying run at Billy and grabs him around the legs. Billy hauls Stevie up feet first and dangles him over his back, threatening to drop him like a sack of potatoes. Stevie squeals and laughs and thrashes at Billy's backside with his fists until Billy lowers him to the ground.

"Stevie, you go on now and see what your grandma's doing," Jake says. He nods toward the house. Stevie kicks his toe in the dirt until Billy bops him gently on the back of the head.

"See you later, Sidekick," Billy says, and Stevie grins and races for the house.

Billy goes back to his work, threads a rag onto a rod and draws it down the long barrel of his rifle. Jake moves over and leans against the workbench. He's chewing on a matchstick.

"Any change today?" Jake asks.

"Not that I can see."

"Grandma still talking about Florida?"

"You know she's just saying that to get me away from Hattie."

Jake chuckles. "She don't like that girl, that's a fact."

"She don't like any girl that likes me."

"I wonder if Alice is going to turn out like that with our boys."

"How is Alice?"

"Aw, she's all right." Jake hitches at the straps of his overalls, shuffles his feet a little. "She wouldn't mind if you'd get into town to see her. Might cheer her up."

"What's she need cheered up for? She's got a new baby."

"Yeah. I know. Anyway. If you could."

"All right. I'll try to get in there."

Jake stands a while and Billy doesn't speak. He knows Jake by now, and he knows if he's got something to say, he'll come to it in his own time.

"Things are changing," Jake says. He claps Billy on the shoulder and moves off toward the house. Billy watches him walk away and shakes his head. Jake hates change, runs from it, and Billy can't seem to find it no matter where he looks.

When Billy goes in for lunch, Grandma sits him down to chicken and dumplings from the day before. She lowers herself to a chair across from him, but she doesn't eat. She never eats until the men are finished, even though Billy has told her for the two weeks that Gramp's been laid up that he wishes she'd just go ahead and eat with him. Her false teeth don't fit too good, her lower jaw slides around and she clatters the teeth together trying to get them lined up right. Billy finds the noise irritating.

"He's got a bed sore," she says. She rests her chin in her hand. Billy looks at her, worried. She seems tired to the bone.

"I'm not surprised."

"Before you go back out, I wish you'd try to turn him over."

"Okay. I'll do that."

She stands and reaches the coffee pot off the stove, pours him a cup.

"Jake was here."

"I know. He stopped out to the shed."

"Stevie's scared of Gramp."

Billy nods his head. "I can see how he would be. Gramp don't seem like himself."

"Jake says if we want to go to Florida, he'll sell the machinery. Give us half the money. He says that's only fair."

"We been over this already."

"I sure would like to go."

"How'll Jake get by?"

"He's got enough to keep himself going. He can lease everything he needs."

"What'll we do in Florida?"

"My sister Sarah's there. She knows people. Help you find work doing something besides farming."

"I thought you might move in with Mary and the girls. Looks like she's staying on at Ordville."

"I might. Later on."

Billy studies the old woman who has raised him. She loves him, he knows that. She's doing this for him, thinking this is the only way he'll get out of here.

"Now that the war's winding down, you don't have to worry about being drafted."

"Hell, ain't nobody going to hire me. I don't even have a high school diploma."

Grandma pats him on the arm. "You got a lot in you. You don't know about it yet, that's all."

She stands then and moves over by the stove.

"We shouldn't be counting our chickens." She nods quietly toward the bedroom door.

When Billy goes in to move Gramp, the room stinks of sweat and urine and old tobacco.

"I'm here to turn you."

Gramp looks at him and nods, breathes heavily. His eyes are rheumy and sad, his cheeks sunken into dark hollows.

Billy works his arms under Gramp's body. He's wearing a nightshirt that rides up and Billy tries not to notice his bare legs, bruised and knobby. Gramp's a heavy man, over 200 pounds, and although Billy strains and tugs and grunts, he can't pick him up. He tries to roll him, but he can't keep Gramp's weight shifted long enough to get something behind him. Gramp lays his hand on Billy's arm, a feeble touch, and Billy stops.

"It's no use, Billy," Gramp says.

Gramp closes his eyes, and Billy leaves the room. He stands a moment in the kitchen, rubbing his left shoulder with his right hand.

"What's the matter?" Grandma asks. "Is he worse?"

"I couldn't do it. He's too heavy."

"Well. That's all right, then."

"It's no use, Billy. That's what he said."

Grandma stops wiping the plates in her hands.

"First time he's ever used my name." Billy crosses to the screen door, lets it bang behind him and goes back out to the shed.

That afternoon Billy drives the old truck into Elmyra to visit Alice. The brick hospital in Elmyra only has eight rooms, four on each side of the front foyer. Alice is in the second room on the left, and he can hear her sniveling before he even gets to the door. She's lying on the bed with Frank propped next to her. She's kissing the baby's face and crying.

"Hang on now, Alice. What are you carrying on about?"

"Oh, Billy," she cries, and she throws her hand out to him and bursts into fresh sobbing. Billy takes her hand and holds it for a minute before he sits down in the chair alongside the bed. He hands her a tissue and she sits up and blows her nose. Frank is sound asleep on the bed.

"Look at him," she says. "He's so little."

"Babies are supposed to be little."

"I know." She's still crying.

"What's the matter?" Billy softens his voice. Alice looks beautiful even though she's crying. Her hair's mussed up and wild around her face, the way he likes it.

"I miss Stevie. Have you seen him?"

"This morning."

"Is he all right?"

"Fit as a fiddle."

"I've never been away from him this long. And they won't let him come in to see me. I ask Jake what Stevie's been doing, but you know Jake. He just says the same old thing, like there's nothing to tell."

"You'll be out of here in no time."

"Billy." She leans over then and whispers to him. Her eyes are frantic, and something crawls along Billy's spine. She's genuinely frightened, and he's never known Alice to be afraid of anything except an occasional rattlesnake.

"What's the matter, Alice? You can tell me."

"Have you seen the papers?" She's still whispering. She points to the *Denver Post* lying on the bedside table. Billy glances at the front page and sees a big black and white picture of dazed soldiers along with victims of those camps, emaciated scarecrows in ragged clothes. The news has been full of what has gone on at Dachau and Auschwitz, names Billy's never even heard before. He stands and folds the paper and stuffs it into the wastebasket.

"You don't need to be thinking about that now."

"It's all I think about. Don't ever be a mother with sons, Billy. It's too terrible."

"Now, Alice. There's never going to be another war."

She keeps on crying, and Billy can't think what else to do except to sit with her. He lets her cry a while, and finally she stops. She flashes a crooked smile at him.

"Something's the matter with me," she says.

"You'll be good as new, once you get home."

"He's cute, isn't he, Billy?" She's picked Frank up now and cuddles him next to her. Even in his sleep, the baby nuzzles at her breast. Billy looks away embarrassed.

"I got to be going."

"Where you off to, so sudden?"

"I'm going to see Hattie tonight."

"My goodness. All the way to Bickford on a Thursday. Must be serious."

"I don't know about that," Billy says, but he grins.

"How's Gramp?"

Billy shrugs. "The same, I guess."

"It's hard on Jake."

"Yeah."

"Jake can't hardly wash his hands without that old man telling him to."

Billy says nothing.

"I shouldn't have said that."

"I never could get close to him."

"He's stubborn."

"Grandma's talking about going to Florida when he, well, if he dies."

"Jake says."

"I don't know if Jake can make it on leased equipment. There's going to be a big farm push with the war ending. Everybody's talking about growth, buying up land. It's not a good time for Jake to be cutting his prospects."

"Well, Billy." Alice's hands pluck at the blanket on the bed. "It's sweet of you to think about that. But you're young. You got a life ahead of you. You can't stay out there on that old place. At least Grandma knows that."

"She don't like Hattie."

"Do you?"

"I don't know."

"Well, then."

"He might not die."

"Probably won't. He'll surprise us all. We'll be having this conversation again next year."

"Yeah, and I suppose you'll be crying."

"Remember when we used to play Kick the Can, when Jake and I first got married? How he'd sit in the house and listen to the radio with Gramp and Grandma, and you and me, we'd go outside and play. Remember that?"

"Course I do."

"We had fun, didn't we?"

"I never could outrun you."

"Laughed ourselves silly."

"You were the best. I was halfway . . . well, you were like a sister to me."

He looks at her, then, straight into her eyes. He falls into the blue pools of them, and she smiles at him. He's got a lump in his throat and his eyes burn, so he stands up and sets one foot toward the door.

"I got to go," he says. "I don't want to keep Hattie waiting."

He picks Hattie up a little after seven o'clock. Under a heavy black sweater, she's wearing a gray print dress, her brown hair tied back and flowing straight and stringy down her spine. A dark mole hovers over her upper lip, and Billy sometimes fixes on that mole, watching her mouth move and not listening to what comes out of it. They ride around in the truck, and then he stops in her dad's back pasture. They park beside a haystack, and for a while they talk about getting out of the truck and lying down in the hay, but it's too cold so they stay put. He slides his arm around Hattie, shoves the sweater aside and edges his hand down the neck of her dress where he feels her breast. She kisses him back a few times, flicking the tip of her tongue through parted lips, her eyes closed. She tries hard, that's what he can't help thinking. She's been through one year of normal training to be a teacher, and he can see it, her standing up in front of a room full of kids getting them to toe the line. Halfway through running his hand up her thigh, he realizes he doesn't want her, not now, not in his life. Not wanting to make her feel bad, he rubs on her a while, and then he says he's tired, it's been a hard week, and he drives her home.

Hattie's no fool, and when she steps down from the truck, she asks him if she'll see him again. "I don't know," he tells her, because he doesn't. He might feel different tomorrow.

"Good-bye, Billy," she says, and he's all but forgot about her before he's down the lane.

He's got a lot on his mind driving home. He's jumbled up about it, wondering why all along he's thought he wanted out of here when this is the only home he's ever known. He drives past the train depot and south toward Courthouse and Jail Rocks before he heads home. He turns off the highway to the base of the sandstone monuments, standing there adrift on the prairie. Moonlight glistens off the rocks and he sits there a long time to think things through. He tries to imagine what it'd be like going through a day without seeing Jake or a Christmas without Alice's apple pie. Stevie would grow up without him, and he'd never even get to know Frank.

He sees how it is, how easily you can lose your place in this world. One minute you're sowing seed in a field in Nebraska, and the next you're overseas liberating some poor devils who've had their lives stolen straight out from under them. He drives home determined to hang onto his life. As soon as he pulls in the lane, he knows it's too late. All the lamps in the house are lit, and Jake's truck is there, and he knows even before he opens the screen door that Gramp has done it, gone and died, had the last word after all and launched him into a life he will have no use for, and it will be a long time, if ever, before he finds his way back home.

# PIPE DREAMS

## JAKE, 1947

When Jake wakes in the morning, he tries to remember why he should get up. There's no field waiting to be plowed, no irrigation tubes to set. He's sold the machinery, all but the beet loader he built with his own hands and the cultivator he not only built but owns a patent for.

"Jake, I got your eggs frying," Alice yells into him.

He doesn't like her eggs. She flips them over instead of drizzling bacon grease on them. The yolks get hard, and he can't stand a hard-yolked egg. Early on, he thought he might get used to them, but he never has. Not in ten years of marriage. It's a little lie between them, and not the only one.

"Jake," she calls again. He sits up. Right where his feet

should go, there's a worn spot in the linoleum straight through to the backing, the pattern skirting under the bed. He slides his overalls off a nail and steps into them. Buckling the straps, he looks at himself in the mirror above Grandma's old dresser. He spits on his fingers and wets down the few stray hairs that cross his balding head. He bumps Alice's green plastic jewel box and topples it over. Folded clumps of waxed paper spill across the dresser. Alice collects hanks of hair, hers and her sisters' when they were kids. The boys' right after they were born, blond curls soft as duck's down. As Jake fumbles to pick them up, he wonders why she's never cut a hank of his hair and wrapped it in waxed paper like a mummy shrine.

This is the old Larabee place, where they're living now. It's nothing but a house on a lonesome stretch of ground. No running water. No electricity. Still, they were lucky to find it, else they would have had to move to town when their lease ran out.

"Jake, your eggs are getting cold," Alice yells.

"Coming."

Jake leans on the edge of the bed and looks out the window. A field from a neighboring farm edges the yard. Maybe in the summer it will be full of alfalfa, and he can smell the sticky purple blossoms. Or maybe corn. If it's a quiet night and there's a breeze, maybe he can hear the cornstalks rustling like his mother's black taffeta dress.

After breakfast Jake finds an excuse to go to Elmyra for supplies. He drives a mile west of town to the cemetery. The first entry has a filigree iron frame over the top, *Oregon Trail Cemetery* looped around inside. Jake turns the truck in at the second drive and winds past the poor people's section. Alice thinks it's a crime the county doesn't mow around these graves. Jake's not so sure. He wouldn't mind being buried beneath the sway of tall prairie grass.

Round the corner is Old Man Melvin's grave, Spud Brody, Jessie McKiddron. Mrs. Heimbuck, who died last year. Jake pulls up by his family's plot. When he gets out of the truck, silence falls down around him like a curtain. It's March, nippy enough for a jacket. The air smells like snapped garden beans. His work boots crunch on the gravel as he walks from the car to the graves. He's careful where he puts his feet. Old as he is, he can hear his mama telling him, Don't you be walking on the bodies of the dead.

Standing on the rise where his father lies buried, he can see Elmyra a mile to the east, rolling hills stretching to Chimney Rock and Mitchell Pass to the west. If he turns north he catches the gray Russian olive borders of the North Platte River. South is nothing but a bank of trees. Further south, thirty miles, is the Larabee place. He can't see it from here. It's in another world.

Gramp's stone is small. Plain, too. Just his name, Thomas Preston, and then the dates. Jake puts his finger out and traces the marking of the year Gramp died. 1945. Rough edges. Two years hasn't been long enough to wear it down.

He'd like to lie on top of Gramp's grave, put his face down in the crunchy grass. Instead, he squats and rests his head against the cool granite. He spreads his fingers on the ground, both hands. Maybe he just wants to feel a growing thing.

"You were wrong, Pop," Jake whispers. He never said this when his father was alive. Couldn't have. "We should have bought land when we had the chance."

On the way home from the cemetery Jake stops at the post office in Elmyra to mail his application for the *Radio Hour* contest. He's been thinking about this contest ever since he saw the sign posted. Winner gets fifty dollars cash and a chance to go on the radio. Alice says they aren't lucky. They could have six entries in the drawing at the Safeway and still not win the giveaway dishes. The way Jake sees it, maybe this is his time. Maybe he can get on the radio show. Maybe they'll have talent scouts from Denver or Cheyenne. Heck, why not?

After he becomes a successful songwriter, he knows what he'll do with the money. He has his eye on a chunk of land east of town with the river running through it and a distant view of Courthouse and Jail Rocks. It isn't but a few acres. He swings by there after he leaves the post office. He pulls off the main road and drives down to the spot he's picked out for the house. He can build their house himself. He'd like to.

He leans his elbow out the open window of the pickup. After checking to see if anybody's around, he opens the door and puts his feet on the ground. He doesn't feel right walking around on land that isn't his, but it feels good to set his feet down on it. He stands and leans against the door of the truck. He shuts his eyes and spreads his fingers to catch the warmth of the sun. He can see the house and see himself building it. He'll put windows on the south facing the Rocks and windows on the north toward the river. No matter where you sit in the house, he'll fix it so you can look outside and forget there are walls hemming you in.

It's time for supper, and Jake stands at the dry sink washing up. He pours water from the boiling teakettle into the wash pan, then ladles in cold water from the pail. He dumps some Boraxo into his palm. His hands aren't greasy, but it's a habit.

Alice is frying potatoes. He smells the onions, hears the crackling.

"We're having eggs again," she says. Jake listens for the tone of her voice.

He shakes his hands off in the wash pan, takes hold of a towel hanging on the wall hook and wipes them dry. He looks out the window. Sun is setting in the west, throwing pink streaks like a game of Pick Up Sticks.

"Frank taking a nap?" he asks.

"Fell asleep on the couch."

"Where's Stevie?"

"Outside somewheres. Can't you see him?"

He peers around the corners of the curtains. Takes in the chicken shed, the outhouse, the pump, the dormant garden, the yard that isn't his. Dirt and a few chickens. Old Rowdy flopped on the ground.

"Nowhere that I can see."

"He'll be along."

"How was he at school today?"

"Stop worrying. He'll be fine."

"That Ralph still pushing him around?"

"I told Stevie to be nice, and then Ralph'd be nice to him."

"We never should have moved here."

"Don't start."

He takes a matchstick from the cupboard. With his pocket knife he clips off the head and drops it in the paper bag that stands by the back door leading to the porch. He sticks the matchstick in his mouth and chews on the end of it. Alice cracks eggs into a bowl at the kitchen table. He leans on the doorjamb, looks over her head into the living room.

"I signed up for that contest over in Sidney."

"That *Radio Hour* thing?"

"Yeh. I figured maybe I could sing."

"That'll be fun. Maybe Libby and Matt will come. It'll be good for you. Take your mind off things."

He shifts the matchstick to the other side of his mouth with his tongue. He wonders why she takes the time to starch and iron the white doilies that cover the arms of the worn couch and chair.

"Did you hear what I said, Jake?"

"Um-hmm."

"Matt says you ought to call soon. They're filling the rosters."

She's talking about that job at the munitions plant in Ordville. It's an indoors job. Stacking boxes and crates. Cooped up all day with strangers. He crosses to the stove and pours himself a cup of coffee. She keeps it simmering on the back burner.

"I could still take that job at the dime store," she says.

"No call for that." He's not looking at her now.

"Just 'til we get back on our feet."

"I saw Trevor Lang the other day." He crosses back to the doorway and leans against it. He's too big for this kitchen. He's in the way no matter where he stands.

"That no account?"

"He's all right."

Alice uses the egg beater on the eggs. Her curly dark hair floats around her face.

"Mabel Frye says he took up with that Endicott girl year before last. Arlene had that new baby then."

"He says he might be looking for a hired hand come summer."

"Mabel says he didn't even have the decency to hide it. Hang his hat on the back door, tell Arlene he was going out, wouldn't be back 'til morning. Whole town knew about it. Arlene with that new baby, and that Endicott girl lording it over her in the Safeway."

"He's hiring."

"Wouldn't it be fun, Jake? Living out there with Libby and Matt so close. And Mary and the girls."

She starts in, then. She tells him how this is a beginning. This is just like opening the first page of a story book. He can't hear her because he's standing on that chunk of ground east of town.

He's looking off toward the river and listening to the wind whistle through a cottonwood.

On the day of the contest Alice throws a fit when he stands in the kitchen in his overalls. "Why do you want to look like a hayseed up in front of all those people?"

Jake doesn't answer. He aims to be himself. If she can't understand that, there's no use telling her.

They pile into the cab of the truck, he and Alice and Stevie and Frank. She bounces Frank on her knees, and they sing their way over the hills. It could be a picnic they're going to instead of the event that will make his life. Alice has on a brown dress with white polka dots, a wide cinched belt. She looks real good.

The contest is held in the Sidney community hall. They have no trouble finding it. Cars and trucks are parked outside for blocks. Inside somebody's set up tables with red checkered tablecloths. A candle sticks out of a bottle in the middle of each table. It's daytime, so the candles aren't lit. A stage fills one end of the room. A wire runs from one side to the other, gray curtains hanging from the wire.

Alice grabs his hand inside the door.

"Don't it look just like a nightclub, Jake?"

He grins. "Like something right out of a picture show." He scans the room for signs of the radio men out of Denver or Cheyenne. He doesn't see anybody looks like a radio man, but they probably don't want to be picked out.

"Better get a table," he says. "I'll see if I got to check in somewhere."

Alice and the boys sit down at a table smack in the middle of the room. He looks around, and just for a minute he feels off kilter. Two women dressed in hats and high-heeled shoes shove past him as they come in the door. They have rouged mouths and new-fangled hair. One turns to the other and giggles when she looks back at him.

"That guy looks like he belongs on the farm," she says.

They laugh at that. He wonders how somebody can say something that is true and, at the same time, make it mean. He runs his hands down the seams of his overalls, makes sure the straps are buckled.

Jake spots a guy in a shiny black suit up by the stage and decides he must be the contest official. He ambles his way around the edges of the room. When he gets close, a lot of people are pressing in on the man, asking him this and that, so he waits. He holds his hat in his hands and turns it round and round by the brim. He glances over at the table and sees Alice talking to Libby and Matt. They've showed up after all. Alice looks up and catches his eye. She makes a face and waves at him.

Finally the guy in the black suit gets done answering questions. He leans on the back of a chair and wipes sweat off his forehead with a handkerchief.

"Say, uh, I was wondering . . ." Jake begins.

"Could you carry these five chairs over to that table by the door?" The man is in a hurry.

"Well, I thought maybe I ought to check in first."

"Check in? Oh. You're one of the contestants?" The man seems embarrassed. Jake can't blame him, mixing him up that way.

"Jake Preston," he says.

"Oh, Mr. Preston. Yes. Well, do you need a place to change?"

"No, sir. This is how I aim to be."

"All right, then. That's your costume, I guess." The little man laughs, so Jake laughs with him.

"You're singing, is that right?"

"Yes, sir. My own songs."

"Good. That's good. Did you bring your own accompanist, or

do you need Janice, here, to play for you?" He motions toward a young woman sitting on a piano bench. She's swinging one leg and popping chewing gum.

"No. I'll sing by myself." Jake shifts his weight from foot to foot.

"All right, then. There's an intermission halfway through, and you're in the second half. Right after the baton twirler. "

"Should I wait backstage?"

"No, no. You can sit by your family. Just come up when it's your turn. I'll be introducing you. Does your song have a name?"

"I figured I'd do two. 'Sandhills Are My Home' and 'Nebraska Sunset.'"

The little man licks the end of his pencil and writes down the names. "All right, Mr. Preston. I'll put down 'Sandhills.' If you win, you can do the other one as an encore."

When Jake gets back to the table, Matt and Stevie are playing a game of Hangman on a napkin. Frank's on Alice's lap, lining up a row of plastic cowboys on the table. Libby and Alice are snuggled up next to each other talking. They're all drinking root beer. Matt bought a pitcher from the window stand on the far side of the room.

"You want any root beer?" Matt asks.

"Don't believe I do." Jake sits down between Alice and Stevie.

"Suit yourself," Matt says. Stevie is just about hung on the word *squirrel.* Matt ought to know better than to use such a hard word with a kid.

"Jake." Alice's eyes are shining. "Guess what Matt's going to do?"

Jake looks at Matt. He looks at his compact body, his thick dark hair. He knows under his shirt sleeve is a tattoo. Matt was a Marine in the Pacific during the war. He never talks about it. Jake can't rightly say Matt lords it over him that he's been in a war and Jake hasn't. He doesn't have to. It's plain for everybody to see.

"I don't reckon I could," Jake says.

Matt looks aside and grins. "I'm thinking about it, that's all."

"Tell him." Alice pokes Matt in the arm.

"There's talk out at the ammo plant. Some of the guys want to build bomb shelters. We'd be a main target."

"You don't say." Jake tries to sound interested. He tries to sound like this isn't the craziest scheme he's ever heard of.

"Emily Fenster said that her daughter's kids, down by Omaha, they have air raid drills in school." Alice flies her hands in front of her face. Jake has pictures of airplanes in his head from watching Alice's hands. "A siren goes off, and then all the kids hide under their desks. She says the kids get scared half to death, but the Offutt base is right there in Bellevue."

"Course we got to move out of Ordville first. There's talk of a new housing development in Sidney, Sky Manor. I think we could swing it." Matt leans over the table, confidentially. "You can't build a bomb shelter in somebody else's back yard."

"Gosh, Uncle Matt." Stevie rocks on his knees. "You going to save us from the Commies?"

"I can't save everybody, Stevie. This bomb shelter's only going to be big enough for my family. Everybody's got to do their part."

"It must be awful expensive," Alice says.

"Not too bad if you do all the work yourself. You dig a big hole and then line it with concrete. Course, you got to have a special sealed door."

"But what'll happen to us if the bomb comes?" Stevie wails. "Daddy, what are we going to do?"

"Pipe down, Stevie." Jake sounds meaner than he intends. The other three turn and look at him. Jake puts his hand on Stevie's head and roughs his hair. "The program's starting now."

The first half goes by fast. There are two ladies with wobbly voices who sing "Whispering Hope." Some kid recites "The

Highwayman" with all the tlot-tlots in the right place. Tap dancers, one old man playing a harmonica. He's pretty good, but Jake doesn't think they'll want him on the radio.

During the intermission Frank gets down to play with some other little kids under the table legs. Matt goes after another pitcher of root beer and takes Stevie with him. Jake starts looking around for the Men's, figures he'll have to take Stevie before the second half with Matt shoving root beer down everybody. As soon as Stevie is out of earshot, Alice turns to Libby.

"Yesterday when I went to pick Stevie up from school, he was backed up against the fence and crying. That Ralph had a bunch of kids gathered around him and was saying awful things to Stevie." This is news to Jake. "I keep telling Stevie to be nice to Ralph, and then Ralph will be nice back."

Matt and Stevie get back to the table right before this last part. Matt, the expert, says, "Stevie, next time Ralph gives you any trouble, you smack him."

"Oh, Matt," Alice laughs. Libby flaps the back of her hand against Matt's arm.

Stevie stares at the floor. Jake takes him by the hand. "Son," Jake says into Stevie's ear. "I got to get some air. How about you come with me?"

Stevie nods, so Jake leads him outside. The afternoon light slants toward dusk. Jake rests his back against the community building. He drapes one arm over Stevie's shoulder, and Stevie leans back against his leg. Some people are outside smoking, but they go in before long.

"Daddy." Stevie's voice sounds high and shaky. "Do I have to hit Ralph?"

Jake studies on his reply. "Remember that old dog Gramp used to have?"

"You mean Filth?"

"Remember how he'd growl at Rowdy?"

"Yeah. Rowdy'd hide under the truck."

"Showing him who's boss, old Filth. He could barely see, but he wasn't going to let some new whippersnapper take over."

"Dad. You think Ralph's like old Filth?"

"Well, son. Matt's right about one thing. There's no sense letting Ralph bully you around. You can't hide out under a truck."

They are quiet a while. Jake is watching some low lying clouds and thinking they might be driving home across the hills through rain. He's hearing the rain patter and wondering how he could capture that in a song.

"Daddy, if I hit Ralph, then will he leave me alone?"

Jake smiles. He swallows hard before he tells his son the truth. "I don't know, Son. It's hard to say what another fellow will do."

The second half of the contest goes by quickly. Jake gets so he can hardly breathe by the time the fire baton twirler is called up on stage. He feels sweat running down his sides, smells himself. He'd like to run out of there, but he doesn't see how he can. The twirler drops her baton twice. The whole audience gasps, rears back in their seats like the fire might stretch out and grab them. Finally, the man in the shiny suit calls his name.

"Go on." Alice digs her elbow into his side. He's glued to his chair.

"Mr. Preston?" The little man waves at him.

He walks up on the stage in a haze. Only other time he can remember feeling like this is when Gramp died. He walked into the room, bent over Gramp's body that they said was dead, and all he could think was: Where's all that fog coming from?

He has to lock his knees together to keep them from banging. His mouth is dry, his lips stick together. He hooks one thumb behind the strap of his overalls and rocks forward on the toes of his work boots. He decides if he opens his mouth, something might happen, so he tries it and a note comes out. He finds that encouraging. Another note follows. He started too high, so he has to stop and start again, but by then he's sure he can get through the song. After the first line or so, it starts to feel good. He remembers when he thought up the song. Warm rain, prairie flowers, lonesome windmill. He aches with the pleasure of remembering, and he sings that ache and when he's done, people clap.

When he gets back to the table, Alice grabs his arm and snuggles up to his side. "You were wonderful." She glitters at him. Matt slaps him on the shoulder. Libby pats him on the hand. Stevie comes over and climbs on his knee. Even Frank grins up at him and holds out one of his cowboys. It's as nice a moment as he can remember.

He thinks for sure he'll be a winner, and he is. Second place. The man in the shiny suit calls him up to the front and gives him a gift certificate for hamburgers at the Fireside Cafe. First place goes to the fire baton twirler. During the applause Jake leans over to the man in the shiny suit and says into his ear, "How you going to put a baton twirler on the radio?"

"Doesn't matter." The man shouts over the noise of the crowd.

"What do you mean it don't matter? That's what the winner gets, isn't it? A chance to make it big."

"KMCB canceled a month ago," the man shouts at him. "Said it wasn't newsworthy."

Jake is quiet on the way home. Both boys have fallen asleep, Frank on Alice's lap and Stevie with his head against her shoulder.

"That crazy Matt," Alice says. "Why would he spend all that time and money building a bomb shelter?"

"I guess it's his way."

"I don't know why they'd even want it. If the whole rest of the world was bombed, I wouldn't want to be left. If you ask me, it's just a pipe dream."

"You sure thought it was a good idea when he told about it."

"I never—"

"You sure did. You were all lit up over it."

Alice turns quiet and stares out the window. Jake looks at the back of her head, her curly hair flying the way it does. He clears his throat.

"He's not hurting anybody, is he?"

"Why are you sticking up for him?" Alice looks at him like his face is dirty.

"I'm not."

"You are, too. And you don't even like him."

"Who says I don't like him?"

Alice laughs at this. It's not a sound he likes to hear.

They ride a few more miles. "I guess I could go on out to Ordville," he says.

She doesn't answer right away. "What about Trevor Lang?" she says.

"I thought you didn't like that idea."

They ride silently, Alice watching out the window. Jake tightens his grip on the steering wheel, glancing over now and then at the back of his wife's head.

When they get home, Alice takes Frank into the crib in their bedroom and he carries Stevie to his bed. Slips off Stevie's shoes and socks, his pants. He decides to let him sleep in his shirt and tucks him under the covers. Jake stands looking down at him for a long time.

When he comes to their bedroom, Alice is already in bed. He slides off his overalls and hangs them on the nail. He moves around through the narrow space between the bed and the wall and sits on the edge where he can see out the window. Alice has her back to him, the curve of her hip outlined under the thin blanket. He puts one hand on her hip and gazes up at the sky crammed with stars, at the Milky Way splayed across heaven like it was swiped with a paintbrush. He thinks about that piece of land with a dry ache. Then softly, so as not to wake her, he lies down and cradles his wife.

# WONDERFUL WORDS OF LIFE

ALICE, 1948

By now Alice and Jake have moved back toward Elmyra, seven miles west of the county courthouse on washboard roads. They live in a migrant worker's shack owned by Carl Rosin who lives thirty-five miles further west down the old Oregon Trail. The adjacent farm, Rosin's farm, is worked by Jude Wentworth, and it's Jude who said they could live here for twenty-five dollars a month. That's highway robbery for a beet shack, but what could they expect from Jude, the same man who once wrote to Gramp's landlord back east in Omaha and underbid the lease so that Gramp was forced to move off land he'd farmed for fifteen years. Alice knows the score on Jude, found it out when she knocked on Carl Rosin's door and asked for money to paint the living room. Mr. Rosin said flat out no, why should he give them money for paint when they were living rent free. Rent free, Alice echoed. No sir, we're paying Jude Wentworth twenty-five dollars a month. Carl Rosin looked her over, disappeared inside his house and came back with a check for ten dollars. Paint the whole damn thing, he said. He never offered to lower the rent.

Jake failed the health exam at Ordville, the government doctor said he had a hernia, and now he's wiring houses up in the Sandhills for the REA. He drives around looking for a house, winds up the long dusty lane, knocks on the door, and asks them do they want to be wired. Most say yes, since it only costs five dollars to sign on. He's thorough and painstaking, having learned how to do what he does from a mail-order extension course from the University of Nebraska. He sends the bill to the REA, and he never cheats, but once the REA refused to pay. Said he way overpriced wiring the Mitchell's house. Jake said he remembered that house clearly, a low soddy stuck back into a hillside. He wrote back and said he'd be happy to take the wiring out, but the Mitchells lived a ways from any power lines and that's what the thing had cost. REA paid, and Alice felt proud of Jake, showing spunk like that. She told him so, placing her small hand on his shoulder. Jake said it was the principle of it. Alice turned away, thinking Jake could stand up for principles better than he could stand up for himself.

Alice can't understand Jake sometimes, how he'll buy a paper poppy or stop on the drive home from Alliance to pick up a soldier hitchhiking, giving away their scanty goods to strangers. At the same time, he's stingy, wanting his home private. If he owned land, he'd be the first to post a No Trespassing sign. Alice isn't like that at all. She'd pool her family with her sister Libby's, if she could. And she thinks you owe it to your family to look out for yourselves first, so nobody else has to look out for you. In short, she likes people more than Jake does, but she's not moved by principles. Together, they may have been the worst choice for Mrs. Foster in her predicament.

It's a sunny day in September and Alice stands in the vestibule of the First Baptist Church, stopped by Mrs. Foster who waited for the last notes of the organ postlude and the pastor's amen before approaching her. The other worshippers have already filed outside. Alice is alone with this woman who clutches her tattered coat around her, several buttons missing, bedraggled hair. She smells like she hasn't had a bath in a while. Alice cradles her new baby, a girl wrapped in a pink quilt, appliquéd angels and *Now I Lay Me Down to Sleep* embroidered in her own hand.

"I always loved that song, don't you?"

Alice can't imagine what Mrs. Foster is referring to, unless she means the closing hymn.

"My mama used to sing that song . . . *sing them over again to me, wonderful words of life.*" Mrs. Foster closes her eyes and drifts dreamily along on the music. Alice grows alarmed, thinking she's trapped here by a crazy person. She clutches her baby tighter. She's heard about people who steal babies.

"Mrs. Foster." Mrs. Foster's eyes fly open, she shies like a deer, and Alice tries to soften her voice so she doesn't spook her more. "What is it?"

"I need to ask a favor." Mrs. Foster can't keep her eyes still, they're roaming around the room, and finally she settles them on Alice's face. "Next Friday. Could you watch my children? There's something I need to do."

Alice's jaw goes slack. Mrs. Foster has three children, two boys and her own baby girl. Alice doesn't even know their names.

"Mrs. Foster. We live seven miles out of town."

"I know where you live."

Alice has heard stories about the Fosters. The husband, if he is her husband, gambles. Travels, too. Why would the Fosters know where they live? Up to no good, she's sure of that. She'd step around Mrs. Foster if she could, but Mrs. Foster bars the way to the door, her arm braced against the stair railing.

"I know it's that road west of town. Out by Degraw School, isn't it? That's what people say."

Alice hesitates and bites her lip. She sees the desperation in Mrs. Foster's face. She watches Mrs. Foster's trembling hand reach out and steady herself against the wall. She's harmless, Alice sees that now. She's harmless and badly frightened, and with that Alice's fear evaporates. She knows Jake will throw a conniption fit, but why should he care, he'll be gone all day. If she can manage three, she can manage six. For a day. It's only one day.

"All right, Mrs. Foster. Bring them Friday."

Mrs. Foster tries to smile, but she's got tears. Alice nods to her. Mrs. Foster reaches out a hand toward Molly, dirty fingernails, chafed knuckles, and Alice is relieved when she drops the hand before touching the baby. Mrs. Foster flattens herself against the wall and Alice sweeps past, careful not to brush against Mrs. Foster's smelly coat.

In Bensons' Store, on the way home from church, Minnie McNealy stops Alice. Her high voice rings out over the whole store. "You be careful with that Mrs. Foster. I hear she's some relation to Mrs. Ewing, over at the Assembly of God church, and you know how those Ewings are."

Eleanor Wood leans over the produce bins. "Her husband is no good. If he is her husband."

Mrs. Benson bumps Alice's arm when Alice holds it out for Frank's nickel ice cream cone. Mrs. Benson has white hair dry as a nest, teeth rimmed in gold. The old woman puts her hand up to shield her mouth and hisses, "I suppose she does the best she can, but have you noticed how dirty those children are? I heard all three have different fathers."

Alice hands Frank his vanilla cone and reaches for Stevie's chocolate one. Stevie stayed in the truck with his dad, holding Molly like delicate china on his lap. Alice licks the chocolate drip that threatens to fall on her fingers. She takes Frank's free hand in hers and tugs him out the door. "Jake's waiting," she says over her shoulder.

On Friday Alice opens the door to Mrs. Foster. Mrs. Foster's holding her baby who keeps reaching to be put down. A man and the two boys wait in a dilapidated car.

"You didn't forget?" Mrs. Foster asks.

"No, oh no. I didn't expect you this early is all."

Mrs. Foster looks as though she hasn't slept in days. She has black circles under her eyes. She waves her hand, and the car door opens. The boys creep out. They're in no hurry. When they reach her, they hide behind her back. She stretches around with one arm and drags them forward.

"This is Martin. He's seven. This is Robert, just turned five. And this is Elizabeth. She's about nine months. Still taking a bottle." She hands the baby to Alice. Elizabeth starts to cry. Alice has to hold her tight to keep her from jumping out of her arms. "Just milk'll do."

Mrs. Foster drops to face the boys and gives each of them a quick hug. She pulls a handkerchief out from the sleeve of her coat, spits on it, wipes at Robert's face. He screws up his eyes and twists away from her. She straightens, her breathing shallow and fast. "Well, you boys mind Mrs. Preston, now."

Women are telling sad stories on the radio to whoops and hollers of a studio audience. Alice turns the radio up loud while she in-

spects the Foster children. Martin and Robert wear faded corduroys with patches on the knees and the butt. The stitches are big
and loose, allowing the patches to curl away from the pants. Their
shirts are not tucked in. No coats. Robert's sweater has holes in
it, probably because Martin wore it first. Shoes scuffed, holes in
their socks. Robert has a cold, his nose red and crusty. The baby
is bald as a cue ball. She's wrapped in a couple layers of outing
flannel. Underneath she wears a threadbare nightdress with the
drawstring missing from the bottom. No booties.

On *Queen for a Day*, the audience gets ready to vote for their
favorite story. Soon everyone will know who wins a new washing machine. Alice hopes it's the woman from Tuscaloosa whose
husband died trying to save the neighbor's drowning dog.

When Mrs. Foster doesn't show up by supper time, Alice starts
to get worried. Jake's tired. Home from a day's work up in the
Sandhills. They get through supper, and then Alice doesn't know
what to do.

"Let's wait a while," Jake says.

At ten o'clock, Alice decides Mrs. Foster is not coming back
tonight. She empties her underwear out of a dresser drawer and
makes a bed for Molly in the drawer. She rocks Elizabeth until
she's sound asleep and lays her in the crib. She finds old pajamas
of Stevie's for Martin and Robert. She lets them sleep in the boys'
bed. She makes a bed for Stevie and Frank on the couch.

"Just one night," she tells the boys.

"Just one night," she promises Jake.

When everyone else is asleep, Alice sits in the dying glow of the
oil stove, her feet pulled up off the cold linoleum. In the dim light
she works on Martin's and Robert's corduroys. She removes Mrs.
Foster's loopy stitches and resews the patches with her own even

buttonhole stitch. She hums softly while she works. When she's done, the patches lie flat. The way they're supposed to.

Saturday Jake goes to town in the morning to get groceries. Especially milk for Elizabeth. Alice looks forward to these weekly trips to town, but she has to stay home with the Foster kids. In case their mother shows up. Stevie and Frank are crabby because she's made them stay home, too. She needs them to play with the Foster boys, although Frank has crawled under the library table and won't come out.

Martin refuses to eat pancakes for breakfast. "Where's Mommy?" He looks at Alice as if she's hidden his mother somewhere. Robert manages to get syrup in his hair. Elizabeth won't sit in the high chair by herself. She throws anything Alice hands her. Alice tries to nurse Molly, but the commotion is too distracting.

Later Alice hauls water from the pump outside and fills a tin washtub. She heats water to boiling in a teakettle and pours it into the tub. She rigs up an old blanket to curtain off one corner of the living room. Starting with the babies, she wrestles all six kids through a bath. The boys wriggle under her hands while she cleans their ears, pours water over their heads. She dresses the Foster boys in old clothes of Stevie's, not the best ones she's saving for Frank, but some play clothes that already have worn knees and elbows. She finds a hand-me-down pair of overalls for Elizabeth. So much water has splashed out of the tub that afterward she mops the floor.

She makes cheese sandwiches for lunch. For supper she boils eggs, fries potatoes, and opens a can of peaches. She hauls more water, heats it on the stove, washes and rinses dishes in two wash pans lined up on the kitchen table. While she feeds the girls, Jake plays Uncle Wiggily with the boys.

By night Mrs. Foster has not come.

"You just let her dump those kids on us." Jake hisses this to Alice in bed. They have to keep their voices down so they don't wake Elizabeth in the crib or Molly in the dresser drawer.

"Not now, Jake."

"What if she never shows up?"

"What was I supposed to do?"

"Did you get an address?"

"No. We've been over this."

"How could you let her leave like that, without telling you anything?"

"I thought she'd be back that same day. She didn't bring a single thing for the kids. Not even an extra diaper for Elizabeth. How could I know?"

Jake turns his back to Alice and pulls the corner of the blanket hard. "Next time somebody asks you to keep their kids, do me a favor. Tell them to shoot me instead."

Sunday morning Alice gets all six children ready for church. She dresses the Foster kids in their own clothes that she washed out the day before. She's sure Mrs. Foster will meet her in the church vestibule, and Alice intends to give her a piece of her mind. Imagine leaving those kids without a word. What kind of mother does that?

Martin has taken to jerking his mouth around, a nervous habit. Robert wet the bed last night. It's the last straw when Jake and Stevie gang up on her.

"Let him stay home," Jake says. "You got your hands full with them others."

"He's not staying home. Get your coat on, Stevie."

Stevie gets his coat, but he stands in the kitchen with it tight against his chest. He won't put it on. "I want to stay with Daddy," Stevie says.

"I want to stay with Daddy, too," Frank wails. He's got a welt on his arm where Robert bit him, his eyes red from crying. His pockets are stuffed with little plastic cowboys he won't share.

"See." Alice turns on Jake. "This is your example."

She turns her attention to Stevie. "Daddy's coming with us."

"Like hell I am." Jake sets his coffee cup down on the red enameled table.

Alice thrusts Frank's arms in his coat sleeves. "Daddy's got to drive. I can't manage all these kids by myself."

"Then I'm waiting outside with Daddy," Stevie says.

"We'll see about that." Alice's voice shakes. "We'll just see about that."


Sunday afternoon Jake puts on his hunting jacket. "Where you off to?" Alice asks.

"Going to walk the fields a bit. Thought I might find a pheasant or two."

"Now?"

Jake faces Alice. "What do you want from me?"

He slams the door when he leaves. Alice watches him cross the yard. She hates the overalls he wears, despises his boots. If she sees his hat hanging on a nail, she will tear it to shreds. The thought of him makes her sick. She sees herself out the door, up the road, swinging her arms. A melody rises in her throat. She breaks into a run, and she doesn't stop, not for him, not for fences, not for ditches, not for miles. She flies out the door like a wild woman, a witch on a broom, her rage rolling her like a tumbleweed. She rises on the crescent moon, she splits into a glowing sun just before she sits down to tie Robert's shoe and read all four boys a story.


Mrs. Foster drives in the yard on Monday afternoon. Alice watches from the window as she gets out of the car.

There's no man with her this time. Mrs. Foster moves slowly. Alice sees the way her arms cradle her middle, the hand she throws out to the fender to steady herself. Walking like she's made of glass, and Alice draws her breath in sharp.

"Boys," Alice says to the room behind her. "Your mother's here."

Robert runs out the door and throws his arms around Mrs. Foster's legs. Martin stands on the front step and bursts into tears. Only then Alice realizes how scared Martin has been, thinking his mother might never come back. Alice places her hand on Martin's back. "Go on, now." She gives him a gentle nudge. "It's all right."

Stevie's at school, so he can't say good-bye. Frank is hiding under his bed, and Alice decides to leave him alone. Alice settles Mrs. Foster in the living room while she fetches Elizabeth from the crib. She grabs the paper sack with the Foster kids' clothes folded neatly inside. She stops to turn the boys' corduroys so the neatly sewn patches don't show. She doesn't want Mrs. Foster to see. Not just now.

"Mrs. Foster, would you like a cup of coffee?"

"Oh, no." Mrs. Foster's eyes are glassy, the sockets dark and shadowed. "You've done too much already."

"The clothes they're wearing," Alice waves her hand, trying to suggest this is nothing. "You can keep them. They're just some old hand-me-downs of Stevie's."

"Boys, will you take this on out to the car?" Mrs. Foster hands Martin the sack. He hesitates for a moment, but when she smiles and nods, his face lights up. "C'mon, Robbie." He takes his brother by the hand.

Alice races through her mind for the proper thing to say, but she can't find it. Instead, she sits down by Mrs. Foster and knots her hands in her lap.

"Your baby sleeping?" Mrs. Foster asks.

Alice nods.

"Sweet," Mrs. Foster says. Alice shrinks from this piling on of pain. She doesn't want to know any more than she has already guessed.

"I'm sorry." Mrs. Foster's voice breaks. Her breath comes out in staccato bursts.

Alice nods. A bit later Alice walks Mrs. Foster to her car. Martin takes Elizabeth on his lap. Robert waves as they drive away.

Alice takes a turn around her yard. She scuffs rocks with her toes. She rubs blue-petaled morning glories between her thumb and fingers. She pulls a few weeds out of the four-o'clocks. She comes round to the drive and looks down the dirt road where Mrs. Foster's car has disappeared. "Damn it all," she says. "Damn it all to hell," louder still, and then she turns away.

# LOST BOY

The car they drive is a 1944 gray Chevy with nearly bald tires. There's a spare in the trunk, but it's so iffy that Jake takes along a repair kit, pieces of tubing, adhesive, a file and sandpaper. He brings a jug of water and an enamel basin for testing the tube, a jack, blocks of wood to brace the wheels. It's a ten-or eleven-hour drive to Omaha, but they won't stop because motels cost money and Jake's appointment at the University Hospital is the next day.

The plan is to drop Jake off and see what the doctor has to say about his gall bladder. Then Alice and the kids will drive home. They can't afford to stay in Omaha, and school starts Monday. After Jake's surgery and his recuperation, he'll take the train home. Dr. Silverman says Omaha is the place for them, the University Hospital, where they do surgeries for families without insurance.

They ride with the windows down, but the hot August wind gusts in, and Alice can't hear herself think. The boys bounce around in the back seat and Molly rides wedged between Jake and Alice in the front. When they can't take it anymore, the boys rig up shades, stripping off their shirts and cranking them into the windows. Frank's shirt, white with red printed cowboy hats, doesn't reach the bottom of the window, so he flops toward Stevie to get out of the glare.

"Get over," Stevie says.

"Stop hitting me," Frank wails.

"Cry-baby," Stevie sings. "Cry-baby, crybaby, crybabybabybaby," until Alice turns around and Jake threatens them.

"Pipe down. If I have to stop this car . . ."

He never finishes his threats. Alice knows it, the kids know it, and within five miles they're at each other again. Stevie only has to look at Frank, screw up his face, and Frank bawls.

Molly rides on her knees, looking into the back seat. She chews on things, her blanket, the tail of her stuffed lion, the top of the paper sack holding her penny candy. When she's not chewing she's sucking her fingers, the middle two of her right hand. Her light brown hair hangs in long curls, the side curls held back by pink barrettes. Tomorrow is Molly's third birthday. Wrapped in the trunk is a new blanket Alice has sewn for Molly's Tiny Tears doll.

At Odessa they stop for a picnic under a cottonwood tree alongside the highway. Jake sweeps the ground of sticks with his shoe and Alice spreads an Indian blanket, faded green and red zigzag stripes on a tan background. She fishes bologna sandwiches and potato chips out of the box she packed early this morning.

"I hate mustard," Frank says and throws his sandwich on the blanket.

Alice picks it up and hands it to Stevie.

"Give him yours. You got the mayonnaise."

Molly picks her sandwich apart, drops the bologna on the ground and eats the white bread.

Jake props his back against the tree, his knees drawn up. Alice sees the worried look on his face.

"Does it hurt now?" she asks.

"Not much."

Jake nibbles at his food. He's afraid to eat since Dr. Silverman said he needed his gall bladder removed. Said that's what's causing all the pain in his gut.

Alice picks up the debris from the picnic and hands around homemade oatmeal cookies.

"I want a drink," Frank says.

He tips the quart jar to his mouth, and Stevie bumps the bottom. Water sloshes into Frank's face, he starts to cry. Alice grabs the jar out of Frank's hand before it falls to the ground.

"Can't you quit picking on him for five minutes?"

Stevie grins and pops Frank on the back of the head. Frank's blond curls wobble in the sunlight. Alice thinks again that she'll have to cut those curls before she takes him to school.

"Jake, can't you do something?"

Jake glances at Stevie. "C'mon, now," he says.

Stevie stops and looks at Jake. Alice watches him looking and wonders what he's thinking. Stevie rubs his lips together and then his shoulders start to droop. "Okay," he says, and he lies down on the blanket next to Alice and shuts his eyes. Molly has climbed on Jake's lap and sits there sucking her fingers. Frank, finally left alone, scoops up Molly's and Stevie's cookies and eats them.

When they reach the edge of Omaha, it's still light, but they spend more than an hour trying to find a motel. Jake wants a place with separated cabins. He can't stand to stay anywhere that has shared walls. One place looks nice, a little creek flowing under a bridge, a playground with swings, but it's too expensive. At last they find the Chalet Inn. Their mock-Swiss cabin has a tiny kitchenette, a double bed, a rollaway for the boys, and a foldout cot for Molly. They're on the outskirts of the city, but the manager tells them it's a straight shot down Dodge Street to the hospital.

Jake asks if there's a nearby grocery that's still open. The manager pencils some directions on the back of a brochure, and Jake brings back milk, corn flakes, a loaf of bread, some cheese, and a few apples. Alice finds a small frying pan under the dirty sink. The gas stove has two burners, no pilot light, and Jake has to go ask the manager for matches. By the time he gets back, Molly has fallen asleep on the bed. Alice has rescued Frank from Stevie holding him down and thumping on his breast bone. Separated, the boys drape listlessly over the ends of the rollaway.

Alice gets a burner lit and fries up the cheese. She cuts the apples and plunks out apple wedges, a glop of melted cheese, a couple pieces of bread on five separate speckled Melmac plates. She uses saucers for two of the plates because there aren't any more dishes in the cupboard. She pours milk into whatever she can find, using a bowl for herself. There's no table, so they sit on the floor and eat their supper. The kids are too tired to fuss. They chew their food in gloom and silence.

After they get the kids bedded down and asleep, Alice and Jake climb into bed. Alice inspects the sheets first to make sure they're clean. They're none too white, but she guesses they've been washed at least. Jake lies on his back and Alice rests her head on his chest, listening to his heart beat and feeling his breath go up and down.

"Jake?"

"Yeah."

"What'll we do about Molly's birthday?"

The silence spreads out. When Jake finally speaks, he sounds like a man who's been hauling wagonfuls of hay for hours on end. "They had some cupcakes in that store."

"Maybe we can find a park."

"My appointment's at ten o'clock."

"We'll have to get moving early."

"She's too little to notice what day it is."

"We can't just skip it." Alice's voice clogs up. "She needs her daddy on her birthday."

"All right, Alice." Jake's big hand fumbles at Alice's shoulder. "Don't worry. We're going to be fine."

The next morning they roust the kids from a deep sleep and prop them up against the walls and coax them into eating cereal. Alice packs the rest of the bread and apples into the lunch box for the ride home. The store opens at eight o'clock, and while Alice and the kids wait in the car, Jake goes in to buy cupcakes. He buys candles, too, and he's remembered to bring the book of matches from the motel. They drive around for forty-five minutes looking for a park. Alice wants to stop and ask somebody, but Jake keeps driving. Finally they find a tiny park with one picnic table perched on muddy ground. There's a swing set, rickety teeter-totters, and the boys race toward them while Alice spreads the blanket on the table. Jake carries Molly over to the swings and sits down in one with her in his lap. Alice can hear his voice singing, but she can't make out the words. She sticks one pink candle in three of the four cupcakes. They're stale, yellow cake with hard chocolate icing. She props Molly's wrapped package on the table. When she's ready, she calls to them: Come and get it.

"How come there's only four cupcakes?" Stevie asks.

Frank reaches for one, but Alice bats his hand away. "Wait a minute. We have to sing and light candles first."

"I want my own," Frank says. "I want one with a candle in it."

"They came four to a package," Jake says. "Mom and I'll share."

They light the candles, and Jake starts them out singing Happy Birthday. Molly's riding in her daddy's arms, her fingers in her mouth. Alice tries to tug them out, but Molly turns her head and rests it against Jake's shoulder.

"Molly, don't you want your present?" Alice coaxes.

Molly shakes her head, and Stevie grabs the gift.

"I'll do it," he says.

"Let me," Frank whines.

"Let Frank help," Alice says, but it's too late. Stevie has opened the package, shaken out the soft blue blanket with white embroidered puppies. He holds it by the top two corners around his neck, scrambles on top of the table, jumps off and yells Superman. Frank laughs and lifts one leg to climb up after him when Alice catches him and hauls him down.

"Give me that," Alice says, snatching the blanket from Stevie. She drapes it over Jake's shoulder and Molly rests her head against it.

"Mommy made this for your dolly," Alice says.

Around her fingers, Molly mumbles, "Where's Dolly?"

At that, Alice realizes they've forgotten Tiny Tears, left her home on the kitchen table. She pats Molly on the back. "Dolly's taking a little rest."

"I want Dolly," Molly cries, over and over, and while Alice and Jake try to comfort Molly, Frank grabs his cupcake and tears the paper off. Stevie takes his time, sticking his finger experimentally in the icing of each remaining cupcake. Jake tries to sit Molly down at the table, but she won't leave his arms. She clings to his neck. He holds a cupcake out to her, but she won't take it. Alice sits across the table and watches her little band. Frank has chocolate icing from ear to ear. Stevie's shoulders are hunched, his back to Frank, feeding himself bits of his cupcake like he's a prisoner in a dungeon hoarding his last meal. Jake has peeled Molly's cupcake and tries to entice her by making goofy eyes at her and smacking his lips. Molly's fingers are in her mouth, her eyes glazed over, head nestled into the blanket still draped over Jake's shoulder. Alice rests her chin in her hands, and thinks, No one will ever love them as much as I do.

They leave the kids in the car with a stack of funny books and a jar of water while they go in to meet Jake's doctor. They've never known a hospital to allow children, and Alice expects to be back within an hour. Jake kisses all three of them, even Stevie, who at ten thinks he's getting too big for kisses. "You take care of your mother, now," Jake says. Stevie ducks his head.

Roaming the corridors of the huge hospital, it takes them a while to find the right department. They're late, but the receptionist says it doesn't matter. She gives them papers to fill out, and that takes a while, too. They discuss what Jake should put down for occupation, and finally he writes in electrician, although he hasn't done any wiring since his stomach started acting up. They give the papers back, and they're told to wait in a room with plastic-covered green chairs. A lot of other people are waiting, too.

Jake checks his pocket watch from time to time, and first one hour goes by, and then another. Every time Alice thinks about going to check on the kids, another doctor steps into the room to confer with a patient or a nurse comes and calls out a name, and she's scared to death she'll miss the moment when it's Jake's turn. She paces and waits. She can't see the car from the window, either, but she knows Stevie's good at taking care of the other two if he has to.

It's almost noon when a woman brings the kids into the room

and asks in a disapproving voice, "Do these children belong to anyone here?" Alice looks up and sees the three of them, all crying, even Stevie, and the woman has them in a huddle with her arm around their shoulders. Alice rushes to them, Jake right behind her.

"We told you we'd be back. What are you crying about?" she says to Stevie. She kneels down and hugs Frank, and Jake picks Molly up. Stevie wipes his nose on his shirt sleeve, his sobs subsiding into loud hiccups. Alice reaches down to smooth his dark shock of hair back from his forehead. The woman stands with her arms crossed in front of her. She's small, silver-haired, and fluffed up like a biddy hen.

"I found them walking up and down the street," the woman says. "I came to visit my sister, and these poor children were wandering around out there. Like lost lambs."

"They're fine," Alice says, straightening up and looking the woman in the eye. "We were right here all the time. Stevie knew where we were."

"Humph." The woman glowers at her. She's wearing a black dress and black hunky old-lady shoes. Her hair's in a bun, too.

"I'm hungry," Frank says, and Alice reaches out an arm to haul his face into her skirt, not removing her eyes from the woman's.

A young woman in a blue uniform comes over and offers to take the children to the cafeteria. The girl kneels down by Frank and says, "Would you like to go have a sandwich?" Frank lights up and takes her hand. The girl smiles and holds her arms out to Molly who miraculously goes to her without a fuss. Stevie stands frozen. His eyes are dried up, and his face is blotchy, and he's not letting his parents out of his sight.

"C'mon, Stevie," Frank says.

"Go on, Son. It'll be all right," Jake says.

Stevie looks at Alice. There's something new in his eyes that she hasn't seen before. She shrinks from it, but she tries to smile at him reassuringly. "What's your name?" she asks the girl. She can read it on her badge, but she wants the kids to hear.

"Cindy." Then the girl turns to Stevie. "I'll bring you right back here. I'll stay with you until your parents are through with your dad's appointment. Okay?"

Stevie moves then. He follows her, but he turns around three times before they get out of the room. Alice watches them go. Jake has already sat back down, and the people in the waiting room are trying to look like they're going about their own business.

Alice sits down by Jake and realizes her knees are shaking. An old man sitting next to her takes out a handkerchief and blows his nose. He opens the handkerchief to see what he's expelled, and Alice sees blood. She thinks about that time the doctor had to pack her nose to stop the bleeding. She'd been pregnant with Molly at the time, only she didn't know it. She's a bleeder, always has been, and suddenly she's frightened for Jake. What if he dies on the operating table? She picks up a *Saturday Evening Post* and tries to read, flipping past ads for automatic washers and dryers, women shown in tidy homes, and she wonders where are these boom times everybody keeps talking about. She flips through the pages, not really seeing, not stopping to read anything but headlines, and finally, after three hours and twenty minutes, the nurse calls Jake's name.

Now she has the kids on the road, and it's midafternoon. She ate a couple pieces of bread and called it lunch, anxious to start the long drive. She figures if she can get as far as Paxton, she can stop at Uncle Henry's over night.

Stevie rides in front with her, his eyes alert and scanning the road. Molly and Frank have fallen asleep in the back seat. Alice thinks she should try to talk to Stevie, but she's scared and doesn't want him to sense it. She left Jake at the hospital, not knowing anything. After all the waiting, all the doctor was willing to say was that they'd need to run some tests. Surgery might be Monday or Tuesday, and because she was nervous about the children, she didn't wait to see Jake to his room. She kissed him good-bye, a peck in front of the doctor and a nurse. Jake squeezed her hand, said he'd telegram when he was ready to come home.

"Don't worry," he'd said, and she tried to flash him her bravest smile.

"Mom, what's that smell?" Stevie asks.

Alice has smelled it too, a hot motor smell, acrid and scorched. She'd hoped it was something outside.

"I don't know."

"There's something wrong with the car."

Stevie's voice edges close to panic. Alice turns to look at him and is alarmed at the size of his pupils.

"Stevie," she says sternly. "It's okay. Daddy checked the car over before we left home."

They are almost to Lexington before the car starts to *chug-chug*. Alice pulls over and wrestles the hood up, and steam pours out from under it. Stevie stands beside her, dancing from foot to foot. "You broke it. You broke it."

"Let me think."

"You broke it. You broke it." Stevie's voice rises hysterically.

Alice turns and grips him by the arm. "Shut up."

Stevie stiffens and except for a small whimper, he goes quiet. Alice feels instant remorse, but she can't think about that right now. She takes her hand off Stevie's arm and looks up the road and down. There's not another car in sight. It must be about five o'clock.

"C'mon. Climb in. I'll drive slow. I think we can get to Lexington."

Stevie rides with his head hanging out the window, as if he might catch sight of the motor going up in flames better from that angle. Molly and Frank are awake and fussing at each other. Alice ignores them, driving with her hands clutched tight on the wheel.

They edge into Lexington. Right along Highway 30, there's Mac's Garage, and Alice pulls off the highway onto the gravel. Stevie jumps from the car like a rabbit. "Frank, you and Molly wait here while I talk to the man," Alice says. She straightens her skirt and smoothes her hair with her hands. She enters the office after Stevie, who is lurking in a corner, pretending to look at fan belts.

The mechanic stands behind the desk in dirty green coveralls. He wipes his hands on a grease-stained cloth. One gold tooth gleams when he smiles.

"I'm having some trouble with my car," Alice begins.

"Sorry, ma'am. I'm closing. Have to wait until tomorrow."

Alice stares at him. "What?"

"Closed. I close at six o'clock."

He walks past her then and flips the sign over on the door. He's whistling. Alice can't quite catch the tune. It seems important to her to know what he's whistling, she strains every nerve toward the melody, it takes up residence in her head. Dazed, she wanders back to the car, opens the door and gets in. At a distance she hears Frank ask her something, and she puts her hands up to her temples and rubs. She's tired, and her head aches.

She's sitting there when she hears the man's boots crunch on the gravel. She hears him, but it doesn't quite register, and then he's at her window. She's startled, afraid, and then she recognizes the man with the gold tooth. He smiles at her and tells her to drive her car on into the bay.

"I'll take a look at it," he says.

"You will?" She's dismayed, and it shows in her voice.

The man leans down and nods his head toward the office. Stevie stands outside watching them, hands thrust deep in his pockets. "Lady. Nobody could turn that kid away."

She waits with all three children in the office while the man checks out the Chevy. Frank hangs onto her hand and Molly leans against her legs, but Stevie stays away from her. He's suddenly interested in car parts, and he wanders up and down the narrow aisle running his hands over pistons and hubcaps. Turns out the Chevy needs a new belt, some water in the radiator. It costs $7.70, and she only has $15, but she's grateful she can pay him. She had already decided that if the bill was too high, she'd have to ask him to trust her to mail it to him. Or she'd have to give him Uncle Henry's address in Paxton.

It's nearly seven o'clock by the time the gold-toothed man is finished, and Alice decides to celebrate by taking the kids to a cafe. They order hamburgers and milkshakes, and she asks for a bowl of soup. The red booth they sit in has tape across the torn seat, the floor of the cafe dirty. Molly dumps her hamburger out on the plate and gnaws at the bun. When the waitress plops her soup in front of her, Alice picks up her spoon. Holding it suspended over the bowl, she starts to cry. Her shoulders shake, and it's all she can do to keep from sobbing out loud.

"What's the matter? Mom? Mom!"

She looks up, then, into Stevie's stricken face. Frank has stopped eating, his hamburger lifted midway to his mouth, lips shaped in an open "o", like somebody out of a cartoon. Alice feels her face breaking apart, not sure whether she's laughing or crying. She points down at her bowl.

"There's a fly," she says. "There's a fly in my soup."

She arrives on Uncle Henry's doorstep at nine o'clock. Thank god, Henry and Norah are home, and they welcome Alice and the kids with open arms and no questions. They find beds for all of them. Alice sings a little song to Molly and Frank, kisses them good-night, and by the time she turns her attention to Stevie, he's asleep on the living room sofa. He's sleeping in his clothes, the sheet pulled up and tucked under his chin. Alice reaches a hand out toward him, but she doesn't touch him. She doesn't want to wake him, and she can't take her eyes off his shoes, the laces tucked inside with the socks, both toes turned the same direction, the heels lined up perfectly even and resting against the edge of the couch.

Henry insists on having their car checked out by his mechanic before he lets them leave the next day. Norah loads them up at breakfast, pancakes and eggs, and then packs a big lunch. She tries to talk Alice into staying on, but Alice wants to get home so the kids can sleep in their own beds before starting school.

Frank begs to ride in front, but Stevie won't relinquish his seat. Alice doesn't bother to suggest that they take turns.

When they hug Uncle Henry and Aunt Norah good-bye, Norah whispers in Alice's ear.

"Quite the little man, isn't he?" and she nods at Stevie.

Alice looks over at Stevie and sees the circles under his eyes, the stoop of his shoulders, the set of his jaw. She remembers the teasing boy he was on the trip down. She thinks about his crooked grin and his laughing eyes. She hears his giggle when he tickled Frank until Frank begged for mercy. She misses him so much, that child she knew in another lifetime, that it's a physical ache, and she puts her hand on her stomach. "Oh," she groans, and Norah catches her by the elbow.

"What's the matter?" Stevie calls, vigilant and accusing.

"I'm all right," Alice says.

And then to Norah, loud enough for Stevie to hear, "I don't know what I'd do without him."

# HOW IS IT WHERE YOU ARE?

JAKE, 1951

J ake's got a lot on his mind while he rides the train home from Omaha. It runs through the night, an old milk train that stops at every station across the length of Nebraska. He shifts to get comfortable in the bench seat, tries to sleep, but it's no use. His arms and legs don't fit, and finally he sits up, leans his head against the glass windowpane and stares out at the thick night.

He can still smell the antiseptic of the hospital. He can hear the tittering of the nurses and the shuffling feet of the orderlies. He got used to having Mr. Doering in the bed next to him, although by the end of the week, he liked having the room all to himself. Especially at night. Mr. Doering snored, which wasn't that bad, but sometimes he cried out in pain or woke frightened and disoriented. Then the nurses would come and sedate him. One night they tied his hands to his bed because he kept tearing at his incision. It nearly set Jake crazy, the thought of being tied down like that. On Tuesday he came back to his room after yet another battery of tests and found Doering's bed empty, the sheets stripped. He didn't find out until someone brought his supper tray that Mr. Doering had died.

"Died?" Jake echoed.

"He had a seizure and was gone. Like that." The nurse snapped her fingers. "It happens sometimes."

After that, Jake took to talking to Doering. He didn't do it out loud, but sometimes, when he felt scared or unsure of himself, he'd think, You know what I mean, Doering. Or walking down the hall, Here we go, Doering. He thought of the old man as a pioneer, someone who had gone before him and understood.

They checked him out for gall bladder first, since that's what he came in for. They x-rayed and poked around and Dr. Freedman told him there was nothing wrong with his gall bladder that he could see.

"That's good news, Mr. Preston. You should be pleased." Dr. Freedman's white teeth glittered, his glasses shone, his bald head gleamed. Like a headlight, Jake whispered to Doering.

"I guess so. But then, why does it hurt?"

"We don't know yet. We're checking out other possibilities."

They made him drink barium and checked his stomach. They tested him for ulcers. He remembered that once a doctor had told him he had a hernia, and they looked for that but found no evidence.

"Is that right?" he asked. "How can that be?"

Dr. Freedman leaned back against his desk, a clipboard in his hands. Jake tried to read the encrypted message on the charted pages, but he couldn't get past his own name.

"Well. These country doctors don't always know."

"It was a government doctor."

"I see. Well. No hernia now."

They sent a sweet-smelling, young blond woman to ask him a lot of questions. She sat with crossed, white-hosed legs, a run in her stocking. See that, Doering, Jake thought, while she wrote his answers down on paper and didn't look up at him. How many bowel movements? Soft or hard? Straining? Was he ever incontinent? Did he have problems with impotence? When did he first notice the pain? Was it aggravated by certain foods? Did eating make it better or worse? God almighty, Jake said to Doering. Can't a man have a moment's privacy?

They brought him food on a tray, mashed potatoes and Jell-O, mushy carrots. Applesauce cake, not too bad. The coffee tasted terrible, bitter and yet watery, but he doused it with cream and sugar.

Somebody wheeled in a cart with books, and Jake chose a Zane Grey western. He lost himself reading about big skies and exploits of men braver then himself. He had no visitors, which suited him fine.

He thought about home, sure. Alice and the kids. He must have missed them, but he thought of them as inhabitants of a different world. In his dreams he moved his family around like checkers on a board. He made Alice young and pretty and not nagging at him all the time. He made his children well-behaved and quiet. Notice how they take pride in their father, onlookers said. He introduced his children to Gramp, raising Gramp from the dead. He made his mother the way she used to be, not the hunchbacked old woman she has become, but the mother who made rice pudding so creamy it melted before your fork touched it.

He began to think of the hospital as home. He surprised himself, since he couldn't get outside. Wasn't he a man who loved the outdoors? Then why did he feel content to lie in this bed, turn the pages of this book, hum a melody inside his head? He wrote down a few words to a song, nothing much, a line here and there about tender walls and freedom blues. Listen to this, he said to Doering.

By Thursday he felt so good that he was sure they'd send him home. He grew frightened at the idea of leaving this new-found womb. What if the pain came back when he was hundreds of miles away from Dr. Freedman?

"What's wrong with me?" he asked Dr. Freedman.

"I don't know, Jake. We've ruled out most things. You're in good physical shape for a man your age."

"My age? I'm only forty-four."

"Yes. And you're in good shape."

"But I have pain."

"Do you have it now?"

"No."

"How about yesterday? Did you have pain yesterday?"

"No."

"When was the last time you felt it?"

"It was real bad the day driving here. And then the day I entered the hospital."

"Um-hmm. But you've felt no pain since entering the hospital?"

"No. Can't say I have."

"Isn't that interesting?"

"Is it?"

"Oh, I was just thinking out loud. Jake, tomorrow I want you to see Dr. Nolan."

"What's he do?"

"He'll talk to you. He's a specialist. Maybe he'll be able to tell you something."

Jake didn't sleep well that night. He had an idea what kind of specialist Dr. Nolan was. He'd already figured out for himself that it wasn't his body making him sick, it was his life, but what was he supposed to do about it? His head, really. He was sick in the head, and he knew what Alice would have to say about that.

He tried to move Alice around in his dreams, the way he had done only days earlier, but he couldn't make her behave the way he wanted. Instead, he kept seeing her that time they visited Denver. She got sick, weak as a kitten, couldn't even get out of bed in the morning. He was afraid she'd bring on another nosebleed. Maybe she was early pregnant. Scared, he'd rustled up a doctor to come to the hotel room. The doctor leaned over Alice with his stethoscope, checked her temperature, took her pulse, pursed his lips while studying her coloring, the pale cheeks, sour breath, then told Jake in a whispered voice that he couldn't find a thing wrong with her. Take her to a specialist, he said, and handed Jake a card. The next morning, Jake got Alice up and dressed, let her lean on him while he helped her downstairs and drove to the specialist's office. They climbed two flights of stairs, Alice so weak she had to stop and breathe on the landings. When they got to the door, the sign said "Psychologist." Alice reared back like a horse about to step on a rattlesnake. "Psychologist? You mean this is all in my head?" Now, now, don't be that way, he'd coaxed her. He believed in sickness in the head, why shouldn't that be as real as sickness in any other part of your body, but Alice wouldn't hear of it. She stiffened her shoulders. Shrugged off his hand. "Let's go home," she said, and she did seem to be cured. Her weakness disappeared. She got out of bed every day and did her chores. She never complained. He watched her for telltale signs, but could see none. Her will power thrilled and terrified him.

Waiting through the long night to see Dr. Nolan, Jake prayed, something he didn't do often. Please let them find something wrong with his body. Something that could be labeled and fixed with surgery or pills. If it was all in his head, what was he going to do about it? The pain felt real. It laid him flat sometimes. He'd read about poor devils who had their legs amputated and still felt a phantom pain. What now, Doering? he asked into the night.

Dr. Nolan, as he suspected, was a head doctor. A psychiatrist. He talked with Jake for a long time. He asked a lot of questions. How long ago did his father die? That was easy. Six years. Had his father been an angry man? Yes and no. Did he feel that he disappointed his father? He didn't think so. Did his mother love him? He supposed she did. What about his wife? She's young. Did he love her? Of course. Why did he give up farming? Lots of reasons, he guessed. Couldn't make it after Grandma and Billy left for Florida. After Gramp died, too hard. The migrant workers came to his fields last because he was a small farmer. Things got bigger after the war; he should have seen that coming. He didn't. He'd thought he could just keep going in a small way. Too hard. Then, hail. And the banker. And Alice. Well, Alice got tired of it all. He had other talents, people said. Alice said. He could learn most things mechanical. Wiring. Plumbing. Cars and tractors. He invented a machine, once. Filed for a patent. No, no he never sold it; he doesn't have a mind for business. People are hard for him. He's shy. He likes working alone. Thought he could write songs. Wasn't that a stupid idea? Man his age. He lives in a pipe dream. Alice says. His kids, he loves them, and worries about them. The world, you know, is not a nice place. But he loves the sunsets, don't you? And then, it's hard to find work. He never really had to before. Never worked for anybody but himself and Gramp. He's not cut out for it. And it's too late. He can't get back what he let go of, that's it. He's lost his best self. It's gone forever, and he's having a hard time coming to grips with that. Other people do. They go through losses and recover. Well, he got out of farming because he failed. He couldn't make a go of it. He got out because he had to. And farming's all he's ever known.

He didn't say any of this to Dr. Nolan, of course. When Dr. Nolan asked, Why did you give up farming, Jake only looked down at his hands. He studied his fingernails for a while. He saw a hang nail on the fourth finger and had to resist the urge to lift it to his teeth and bite it.

"Mr. Preston?" Dr. Nolan urged.

Jake looked at him then. He looked at Dr. Nolan's narrow pinched face, his eyes boring holes in the air, the mole on his chin with two whiskers protruding. "I can't rightly say," he told the doctor. "Just seemed like the thing to do at the time."

Alice is waiting at the depot early Tuesday morning with all three kids. He steps down from the train and his heart opens to them, his loved ones, and he wraps Alice in his arms. He scoops Molly up, rubs the top of Frank's head. Stevie stands back, out of reach. On the way home, Frank chatters on about school, first grade, already he can read, wanna hear him recite the pledge of legions? Alice tells him the news from town. Stevie rides in the back without saying a word.

After Stevie and Frank have left to walk the quarter mile north to Degraw School, Alice settles Molly at her little desk with paper and crayons. Finally she turns to him.

"Well, what did they say? Your telegram said no surgery. What happened?"

He rises from the table and pours himself another cup of coffee. Adds cream and sugar, the way he likes it. He stands with the cup in his hand, smells the rich aroma and thinks, Now this is coffee, Doering. He feels the cramping in his abdomen, but it's not real. A phantom. He ignores it.

"They kept you ten days. What was that for?"

They hadn't, of course. They'd discharged him Friday morning, after his fruitless talk with Dr. Nolan. They gave him a list of head doctors in his area, the closest in Cheyenne, as if he could just run there any time he felt like he might explode. Or disappear.

He'd wandered about dazed for hours. He remembers now a big park, a street named Dundee, little else. He'd actually stepped into a bar, envious of men who could find solace there, but it was foreign to him, the whole atmosphere of smoke and the wooden stools and glistening bottles behind the bar. He'd stood in the doorway a few moments, then turned and left again.

He wandered into a church, amazed to find the door unlocked in this big city. Don't they worry about vandals? he whispered to Doering. The afternoon sun slamming through the stained-glass windows hurt his head, the profusion of color running riot over his senses. He sat in back and rested his brow against the pew in front of him. He sat that way for a while, then rose up and saw a crucifix in the front of the church. Catholic, then. Oh-oh, Doering, we're in the wrong place. But he stayed. An organist came in to rehearse, and big round sounds floated through the sanctuary and after sitting there for a long time, his heart grew quieter. The flutters in his head subsided, and he could think a little clearer.

On the way out he picked up a brochure that listed shelters and cheap places to stay the night, a YMCA only a few blocks away, directions printed on a tiny inset map. Dollar fifty a night. Why not, Doering, and with that, Jake found himself a room with a small cot and not much else. Bathroom down the hall.

The next two days remained fuzzy in his head. He knows that he walked the streets during the day. He must have found something to eat here or there. How is it where you are, Doering? That was his primary question, and he did everything he could to open himself to the answer. He waited for Doering to speak to him, to send a sign. He looked in reflections of storefront windows, listened to overheard snatches of conversation. He knew the sign wouldn't come to him in a miraculous bolt of lightning, nothing that drew that much attention. Maybe in some underlined verses of the Gideon Bible in his room. Penciled at the bottom of a discarded newspaper on the table where he had his morning coffee. For two days he wandered and waited and he heard and discovered nothing.

The nights were the hardest. When he sat on the edge of his cot or lay down, he thought about how he might actually do it. End. He thought of methods. Played with them, really. That's all it was. A bridge. A miss-step into the traffic. He'd want it to look like an accident, if he could manage it. He wouldn't want Alice to know. Or the children.

In the night his hands grew sweaty and his pulse raced. He felt paralyzed and helpless, lying without volition on his little cot far from home. He recognized his symptoms, diagnosed himself as a man terrified. And finally at long last, Doering came to him. Sat on the edge of his cot and nodded his head.

Tell me, Doering said.

I don't have it, Doering. It's not in me.

What don't you have?

Whatever it takes to make a life. It's lacking. You understand, don't you, Doering?

It's easier than you think.

Dying?

Dying and living, happening all the time.

What shall I do?

Go to sleep. And in the morning, get up.

On Monday, without knowing he was going to do it, he walked to the telegraph station and sent a wire to Alice. *No surgery. On the morning train. Love, Jake.* He walked to the train station and bought a ticket and sat on a bench and waited. Thanks for nothing, Doering.

"They kept you ten days, Jake. What was that for?"

"Tests."

"What tests?"

"What's up with Stevie? He wouldn't even look at me."

Alice twists her hair between her fingers. She does that when she's nervous. "He's all right. You know kids."

"He seems different."

"He's just growing up. That's all."

"He's kind of distant."

"Jake. What did the doctors say?"

He sits then and puts his cup on the table. He reaches across for Alice's hand. "They couldn't find anything wrong."

"They . . ." Alice pulls her hand from under his and sits back in her chair. "What's that supposed to mean?"

"I don't know. A fluke of some kind. I'm fine."

"No gall bladder problem?"

Jake shakes his head.

"What about that hernia?"

Jake shakes his head again.

Alice stands and takes a turn around the table. He can see her thinking hard. Long as he's known her, he can't predict what she'll do with this. He only hopes she'll find some way to think about it that lets them go on.

She stops behind his chair and puts her hand on his shoulder. When she speaks, he hears a quiver in her voice. "That doctor at Ordville . . . and Dr. Silverman . . . they saw something. They must have. And now it's just . . . gone?"

"I guess they were mistaken. All along."

He waits for her to withdraw her hand from his shoulder, but she doesn't. When he's sure she's not going to bolt, he reaches up and takes her hand, leads her around in front of him.

"Do you still hurt?" she asks.

"Not much."

Then, as if he's been planning it all through the long night, he tells her what he's going to do. "I'm going back up there and apply at Ordville."

"You are?"

"The only thing stopped me before was that hernia."

Gently he coaxes her onto his lap. With her face inches from his, lips wide, he says, "We're going to be all right." She folds then, sighs deeply and nestles her head onto his shoulder. He squeezes his eyes shut tight and breathes in the scent of her. His hands betray a slight tremor, but he says it again. "We'll be all right."

# FIBBER MCGEE'S CLOSET

## STEVIE, FRANK, AND MOLLY, 1952–1956

The piano. Jake buys it for fifteen dollars at a farm sale advertised on the highway to Ordville. He works there now, passed the physical, no problem. Libby and Matt have moved into Sidney, a new development of 1950s tract houses that Jake and Alice can't afford, so they have stayed put in their rented house west of Elmyra. Jake rides in a carpool with Gabe Lopez and some other men, and it's Gabe goes with him in the old truck to bring the piano home one Saturday.

An upright player piano. Dark-stained, not a scratch on it, although the varnish is thick and warped in places. Jake shows Alice and the kids how the doors slide open to reveal the apparatus where the scrolls fit. He opens a red-stained, hinged bench that houses dust and cobwebs and two paper rolls with holes punched. He kneels under the keyboard and swings out the foot pedals. After fitting the rolls inside the casings, he sits down at the bench, pumps his feet on the pedals, but nothing happens. The mechanism's broken, and the family sighs with defeat until Jake plays "The Tennessee Waltz" by ear, sweeps Molly onto his lap and lets her hands ride his fingers while he pounds out "Peter, Peter Pumpkin Eater" on all black keys.

That train table, too. Jake built it out of plywood, four feet by eight feet, and when it's up during the few weeks before Christmas, it completely fills the living room, all the furniture pushed back against the walls. Molly and Frank stand for hours, noses pressed against the table edge, watch the twin Lionel engines round the corners, hold their breath to see if the plastic doll they've laid on the tracks will make the cars derail. Jake's handmade depot straddles the tracks, the train tunneling under the red roof and through the silver walls. A light switch blinks, stop and go. Magical, magical, and they load flatcars and oil cars with Tinker Toys and plastic people who ride to kingdom come and back again. Smell the oil and metal; see the sparks shoot out, careful, careful now, up over a bridge, the track wobbling on stacks of loosely piled blocks. Hours fly by, oh, the fun they have with that old train set, these children, so fortunate to have a dad who can make anything, a mom who will turn the whole house over for weeks at a time.

Decorating at Christmas. Aerosol-snow bells and angels stenciled on the windows, the tree bubble-lighted, roped with looping beads and draped with icicles, don't toss them in a bunch now, hang them long, silver, and shimmering, to cover the airy spaces of the Douglas fir.

Alice takes a job as a Stanley dealer and loves it. She drives around the panhandle holding Stanley parties in women's houses, selling Germ-Trol and Try-It and Cool-a-Ped, mops and brooms and bubble bath. Paid for having fun, and she wins prizes, a horse lamp topped by a red, black-fringed shade, a mirror with flamencos painted on it, a set of dishes, a sterling silver service for eight in the King Cedric pattern. She wins gold cups and trophies and lines them up on top of the piano. She works when the kids are in school or takes Molly with her in the summer, singing in an off-key voice as they bump over washboard roads so that Molly, who has an ear for music, learns the tunes wrong and doesn't know it until years later when she resurrects Jake's homemade family records and howls at the way she butchered "Away in a Manger."

The games: Monopoly and Clue. Molly, too young to play, sits at the table watching. She's allowed to take the black Clue packet into the storeroom, pull the string on the naked bulb, slip the cards out and see who's guilty before the game starts. She watches while Frank accuses Colonel Mustard, knowing Professor Plum did it with the candlestick in the ballroom, but she never gives away a thing. Not so much as moves a muscle. If she does, they'll play without her, and she doesn't want to miss out on the fun, even though it's not much fun to sit and watch. Still she watches them having fun and thinks, I'll play when I get big enough, except by then it has all fallen apart, the games, the electric train, even the piano strangely silent.

It begins with Jake's obsession over a young woman at work. He talks about Rebecca constantly. She works in the same bunker he does. She's slight, young, needs somebody to look after her.

"You're in love with her," Alice says. The children, hiding in the boys' bedroom, hear the sneer in her voice.

"I want to adopt her," Jake says.

Alice slams the frying pan down on the stove top. Hands on

hips. Flaring face. "You don't adopt someone twenty-two years old, Jake. You marry them."

"She's a kid. And alone."

"Choose. Her, or me and your children."

A few times Jake slaps Alice in the face. She goads him, it seems to the children. She stands up to him and tells him he's stupid, and they want her to stop, but Jake reaches out and slaps their mother, and their cheeks smart. Please, please, Molly begs in the night. She sleeps in a crib in her parents' bedroom, and one early morning she wakes to strange sounds. A single beam streaks under the window shade, and she sees Jake turn Alice over his knee and hit her with his flat hand. His hand moves through the air as big as the wing of an airplane. Molly pretends to be sleeping, and Jake roars from the room.

All day Molly crouches outside Alice's bedroom door and listens to her crying. Late in the afternoon she creeps in and wipes the hair away from Alice's tear-stained cheeks.

"What's wrong, what's wrong?" Molly repeats over and over, until Alice turns a brittle face to her.

"Nothing. Now leave me alone."

That night Alice makes a bed for Molly on the red couch. She lays a blanket on the arm, Molly's yellow dog and purple rabbit stretched foot to foot, another blanket over them. After her mother kisses her good-night, Molly grabs her doggie and bunny, stacks one atop the other and cradles them in the crook of her arm. What did I do wrong? she wonders. Why does my daddy want a different little girl than me?

They go on every day as if nothing has happened. Alice smiles at the children and jollies them through supper. Jake grows more silent, lurking in the shadows of their lives, coming and going at odd hours, following them to church on Sunday in the old truck.

"You're seeing Pete Rittenberg," he accuses Alice.

"What does he mean, seeing?" Molly whispers to Stevie. The three children are sprawled on Stevie and Frank's bed. The room is tiny, Grandma's old four-poster sandwiched between the wall and a gun cabinet, an upright wardrobe and a beat-up dresser flanking the few feet of open space in front of the door. They hear everything being said in the kitchen.

"Sh-h-h," Stevie says.

"Don't think I don't know what's going on," Jake says.

"It's your sick imagination," Alice shouts.

"I saw you."

"What did he see?" Molly asks.

"Nothing," Stevie says.

Frank is lying on his back, playing with a string looped through a button, pulling the ends of the string so the button zings like an accordion. "He's crazy," Frank says. He shrugs and pulls again on the strings.

Molly starts to cry. Both brothers ignore her, and Stevie turns up the radio.


The summer that Molly is moved out to the couch, Stevie comes home from the river one day with seven baby raccoons. Eyes still shut, furless and scrawny. Rowdy had raced ahead through the prairie grass, surprised the mother who turned on him. By the time Stevie got there, the dog had killed the mother raccoon, and Stevie wrapped the babies in his shirt and tied the sleeves like a sling to the handlebars of his bicycle. He rode home in a frenzy, and now he stands like a supplicant and waits to see what his mother will say. Alice tosses him a cardboard box, Keep them out on the porch.

Their parents fight about this, too.

"We'll have raccoons running all over the place." Alice's voice rises in a shriek at the end.

"We won't have raccoons."

"We will if they live. What then?"

"Keep your voice down."

"I won't. You aren't the one who has to deal with the things these kids do."

Stevie sets his alarm and gets up every three hours at night. He sits in the dim light on the porch and holds each baby raccoon in his hand and tries to force milk down its closed throat. He commandeers Molly's doll bottles, experiments with different-sized holes in the nipples, ruins them one by one. He finds an old eye dropper. He dips his finger into a glass of milk and offers it. Nothing works. Every day, sometimes twice a day, Stevie digs a hole out by the shed and buries a tiny carcass. The first one he lays in carefully, Molly teary-eyed and clutching his shirt-tail behind him, but by the fourth or fifth, he doesn't bother to stoop over, just pitches in the body and stomps the dirt down with his bare feet.

"Why'd they die?" Molly asks.

"How should I know?" Stevie shoves her a little when he walks by to put the spade back in the cellar. He's sick of her questions. There's nothing he can do. Nothing.

One day Jake comes home from Ordville early. He's upset, and the children stay out of his way. They loll outside on the steps, afraid to go in and afraid to wander too far. At last Alice drives into the yard in their battered Buick, and the kids rush out to meet her. "He's home," Frank says. Molly grabs her mother's hand. Stevie takes the Stanley suitcases. They escort her as far as the steps to the house where Frank and Molly stop. Stevie goes all the way to the porch where he drops the suitcases and scuttles back down the steps.

"He's just sitting with his head in his hands," he tells Frank and Molly.

"Lift me up," Frank says.

"They'll see us."

"No, they won't. Put me on your shoulders."

Frank stands on his brother's shoulders, peers into the kitchen window and sees his mother walk over to the table. Jake looks up with red-rimmed eyes. His thin hair stands up around his balding head. His glasses are on the table, and he looks strange to Frank without them.

"What is it?" Alice asks.

Jake doesn't answer.

"Jake?"

"She's gone," he manages.

"Your mother?"

Alice's voice sounds soft, and Frank thinks, oh, Grandma died. She could, she's old and creepy. She lives in a sour house with Mary down in Sidney, two old women in that tiny apartment, the bedroom stinking of camphor and ear wax. He's thinking about the pillowcase his Grandma embroidered, a long red train and yellow daisies. He's thinking he'll save that pillowcase forever when Jake finally raises his head.

"Rebecca," he whispers.

Alice sits back hard in her chair. "Don't tell me this. Don't you tell this to me."

"I got no one else to talk to."

"Get out."

"Where?"

"I want you to go. Get out of here."

"Where can I go?"

"I don't care. I just want you gone."

Alice stomps from the room and Jake keeps on sitting at the table. Frank motions for Stevie to set him down. Stevie lowers Frank to the ground, and Frank takes off running. "What happened? Frank? Frank?" Stevie calls, but Frank can't hear him. He's already down the lane, heading a quarter mile up the dirt road, through the school yard and behind the coal shed where he stops and hugs his stomach. He picks up the largest rock he can find and pitches it at the back of the shed, splinters the old wood, and then he picks up another and throws again, and he throws until his arm is sore and his throat hurts and the back of the shed looks ragged and there's a sizable hole broken all the way through.

Later after supper, when the fireflies have come out, Frank makes his way back home. The car is still in the drive. The old truck, too. He walks onto the porch and holds his breath. The radio's playing, and in the living room he can see Jake reading in the red chair by the horse lamp. His parents' bedroom light is on, so he guesses Alice is lying down. She gets tired.

He hurries through the living room without looking at Jake, opens the door to his bedroom where Stevie and Molly are lounged on the bed playing Crazy Eights. He flops down on the foot of the bed, scattering their cards every which way.

"Look out," Stevie says.

Frank offers nothing.

Molly puts her hand on his knee.

"What'd they say, Frank?" Stevie asks.

He's on his back, eyes open wide, staring at the ceiling. He decides to tell them the truth. He sits up and shakes his head. "I don't know."

Not long after Stevie's raccoons die, Frank practically moves in with a migrant worker family. Stevie meets Roberto first, comes upon him in the schoolyard where they've both gone to target shoot. Roberto has a brother Miguel, Frank's age. Frank spends hours at the beet shack where the Morales family lives, the mother patting tortillas between her palms, Spanish singing through the air. Frank sits at the table and repeats the words they tell him, *mofeta, caballo, gato*. He has no idea what he's saying, but he doesn't care, it's a relief to be bathed in their laughter. He sinks his teeth into the soft tortillas, watches Miguel's father who cannot speak a word of English and copies the way he rolls his tortilla to scoop up beans. There are sisters, two of them, one older and one younger than Molly, with black hair and shining eyes. The girls are too little to go back and forth, but Frank tells Molly of Mardelis and Rosa when he comes up with his plan.

They use their wagon. Stack it with toys, Molly's newest doll, the gun and holster set Frank got for Christmas. They would have added the electric train except that Miguel's family has no electricity in their shack. Balls and airplanes. The air rifle. Games—Clue and Monopoly. All the things they have no use for. Miguel has toys back home in Texas, Frank explains to Stevie, but he can't bring them. So, they pack the wagon and the boys are set to haul it a mile down the road when Alice intercepts.

"Here. What are you kids doing?"

"Sharing some stuff." Frank uses the word *share* on purpose.

"That's Molly's new doll." Alice rescues Betty off the pile. Molly stands nearby, fingers in her mouth.

Alice picks off the newest toys, the family games. There's a small pile left, only their oldest and tackiest things, broken even, but the boys trudge off with the wagon. On the way they steer toward the dump, third tree from the east on the rise, where everybody drops their threadbare couches and broken down wringerwashers, and there they tip the wagon and watch their old things roll into the ditch.

They try to save birds dropped from nests. They seine dirt for their road graders and relocate the cutworms instead of stomping on them. They chase after dragonflies and butterflies, but let all their captives go. Frank and Stevie mope for days when the Morales family leaves for Texas amidst promises to "see ya" next year. That fall when frost threatens, Frank steals into Alice's closets and takes out all her sheets and drapes them over mounds of four-o'clocks and zinnias, night after night until Alice makes him stop.

Stevie gets an after-school job doing chores at the Gibsons' up the road, so Frank and Molly take to baking mountains of cookies, snickerdoodles and chocolate chip and gingersnaps. They pile them on the cabinet counter to cool until Alice gets home exhausted from driving around the panhandle. They hand her cookies, and she smiles at them. The next week they throw out the stale cookies and start over again.

At night the three children huddle on Stevie and Frank's bed. They listen to *Fibber McGee* and *The Lone Ranger*, and Molly has to promise not to get scared or they won't let her stay during *Mystery Theater*.

"People go through hard times," Stevie explains.

"On purpose?" Molly asks.

Frank holds his hands over his ears. He doesn't want to hear this.

"Dad's been laid off. The government is shutting down Ordville."

"Uncle Matt's still got a job." Frank lifts his hands off his ears when he says this.

"That's because he does the plumbing and stuff like that. They aren't going to store ammunition anymore."

"I hate Ronnie Techner," Frank says.

"Me too," Molly adds.

Ronnie's the kid at school who got his leg burned badly last year, who cries to get his way, who whines about every bad little thing that happens to him.

"Sh-h-h," Stevie says. "Here comes the good part."

They lean in to listen, barely breathing while Fibber makes his way to his closet. Don't do it, don't do it, don't open that door, but of course Fibber does, and debris pours down on his head, galoshes and board games, smelly tuna fish sandwiches, baseballs and orphaned gloves, the clatter goes on for minutes and they picture it, the whole sky raining down on his head, and they laugh until they are rolling and tumbling and can barely manage to stay on the bed. Nothing could be funnier than this little man who never quits, never, never, just keeps on opening that door, and next week he'll be back to do it all over again.

# SECRETS

The day that Jake locks himself in the car, Alice bakes a cherry pie. Matt and Libby and their four kids are due for dinner, and Matt loves cherry pie. It's a Saturday, Easter weekend. Molly, Stevie, and Frank have been busy all week dying four dozen eggs. They've redipped and overdyed until most of the eggs have turned murky brown or khaki green. They're outside hiding and hunting the eggs when Jake comes home. He's working for Albert Cochran now, about three miles away, and he's been helping Albert through the morning chores and tinkering with his John Deere to get it up and running for spring.

"Albert sent milk," Jake says, setting a gallon jar on the kitchen table. The milk glistens blue and watery, heavy cream floating on top. The kids hate this milk, call it cow's milk as opposed to the homogenized town milk they prefer, but they need the supplement to Jake's meager wages.

Alice studies him out of the corner of her eye while he washes up. He pours water from the chipped enamel pitcher, dumps Boraxo into his palms. He's quiet these days. Ever since he started weekly visits to a chiropractor in Cheyenne, he doesn't have those fits of anger. She thinks of those bad months as his spell, when he was not himself, and she's glad to have those days behind them. Still she watches him warily. He moves slowly. Sometimes his hands tremble.

She rolls the pie crust out on the table top. Her arms move in practiced strokes, forward and back, around to make the edges smooth. The ceramic rolling pin clatters and *whirrs*, flour dusting the red Formica tabletop. She'll put the leaf in the table before dinner. The kitchen will be cramped, the deep freeze taking up one whole wall. The freezer's full of pheasants and ducks Jake and the boys have shot, chickens they raised themselves, corn from Albert. It all helps.

"How'd it go today?"

Jake raises his head but looks at the wall in front of him when he speaks to her. "Oh, Albert. He lets his machinery go to ruin."

"Doesn't know any better, I expect."

"He's running that place into the ground."

"He is who he is, Jake. You got to learn to accept things."

She turns the pie crust into the glass plate and drops a clump of dough to roll the second crust. Jake grabs the towel hanging on the wall rack and dries his hands.

"What time are Libby and Matt getting here?" he asks.

"I told them anytime. Just so we're ready to eat at noon."

"It'll be a madhouse."

"A little commotion won't kill you," Alice says, but Jake has already moved outside. She smells her cherry pie filling boiling over on the stove and grabs the handle without a hot pad. Damn, she says softly and holds her burnt thumb to her mouth.

When Libby and Matt arrive, their four kids spill from their car. Jim's one year older than Molly, Susan a year younger, the two little boys, Greg and David, six and two. Libby picks David up, but the others run wild as soon as their feet hit the ground. They race in circles around the shed, the chicken coop, the outhouse, the old horse tank and the windmill. "You kids stay out of those haystacks," Alice warns. The hay belongs to their landlord, and he doesn't take kindly to having it scattered to the four winds.

Alice has promised Stevie he can leave after dinner to see his friend Jerry who lives five miles north on dirt roads. She doesn't know what she'll do about Frank. Ever since Stevie's gotten a school permit, Frank pitches a fit any time Stevie wants to go somewhere without him. Still, Jim won't like it if Frank leaves, and why should he? They don't see that much of each other, and cousins should know one another.

"Frank, go tell Dad that Libby and Matt are here."

Frank glowers at her. She knows what he's thinking. She always knows what Frank's thinking, maybe because he's the most like her. Jake's under the house, in his cellar, poking around with his tools. There's no way that he didn't hear the car pull in the drive. Plus, the dog's barking his head off. Of the three children, Frank seems to be the one who can't forgive his father for those bad times. Frank opens his mouth to say something, and Alice waves her hand. "Go on. Tell Daddy."

Frank stomps off in the direction of the cellar. Alice throws her arms around her sister. Libby's wearing a pink dress with a white cardigan sweater, clip-on earrings that look like tiny baskets of pink flowers.

"You're getting so skinny," she laughs into Libby's ear.

Libby holds Alice at arms' length. Alice is suddenly conscious of her green print housedress, her fleshy stomach. She puts her hand at her thickening waist and says, "It's all those Stanley hostesses feeding me fancy desserts."

Matt stands in the yard, adjusting his pants after the long car ride. He's got a big goofy grin on his face, the way he always does. He lights up a room just by walking in, and Alice thinks Libby's lucky to have found a man with such a sunny disposition. Molly's showing Matt the basket of eggs.

"Gorgeous. Beautiful. Oops, that one's got a crack in it. How about if I hide these for all you kids?"

The kids jump up and down, hollering, all except Stevie who looks like he'd rather disappear. "Stevie can help me," Matt says, and Alice thinks again, what a guy.

Frank comes around the corner of the house, a dark scowl on his face. He looks straight at his mother. "I told him."

"Hey, Frank," Matt calls. "You want to help hide eggs with me and Stevie or hunt them with the other kids?"

Frank's blond head bobs while he thinks this over. "Hunt, hunt," Jim prompts, no doubt counting on Frank to know all the best hiding places.

"Hunt, I guess."

The kids troop toward the house to make sure they can't peek while Matt and Stevie hide the eggs. Matt, thoughtful again, says, "Why don't you kids go wait in the shed? I bet Alice's got her hands full in the house."

Alice and Libby check on the ham baking in the oven, situate David on the floor with a toy truck and a red tractor. Then Alice pulls Libby off into her bedroom. She takes an envelope out of her dress pocket and hands it to Libby.

"Is it bad as the last one?" Libby asks.

Alice nods her head. "What are we going to do?"

Libby unfolds the thin onionskin paper from their sister Grace. She's married to a farmer and lives far away in Iowa, and her letters are full of horrors. Herman hits her, blackens her eyes, once he chased her with a knife and ran her straight into a maple tree. She broke her nose, and it took weeks for the swelling to go down. There are hints that something's going on with Herman's sister Ruby, who he lived with before meeting Grace in Denver.

"What's this stuff about Ruby?"

"Keep reading."

Something's odd about Ruby, she floats down her stairs in a nightdress when Grace and Herman go to supper. Sometimes, Grace writes, Herman disappears up the stairs with Ruby for over an hour. Libby reads the letter, exclaiming over Grace's cryptic note. "Oh, no. My gracious."

She finishes the letter and Alice takes it back from her. Alice waits for Libby to think it through.

"You don't think . . .?" Libby pauses, unable to say the words.

"No. His sister?"

"She's sickly, isn't she?"

"He's always taken care of her."

"Both their folks are dead?"

"Car accident. Grace says Herman's all the family Ruby has."

"Well. I never. Ruby's jealous, for sure."

"Libby, what shall we do?"

Libby sits on the edge of the bed, slips her white flats on and off. One of them gets away from her and she stretches her leg to retrieve it. Alice, standing in front of her, grows impatient.

"Libby!"

Libby straightens up, runs her hand over her bubble hair-do. She looks Alice in the face and bunches up her eyes like she's concentrating.

"He doesn't bother the kids?" Libby says this as a question.

"I don't think so. At least Grace's never mentioned it. I don't think she'd stand for that."

"I never thought she'd stand for any of this."

"What's she supposed to do?" Alice's chest feels tight, like something's stepped on it and squeezed all the air out.

"She could leave him. I would. I'd never let a man slap me around."

Alice turns her back and slips Grace's letter into the plastic jewelry box that sits on her dresser. "That's easy for you to say, Libby. Matt wouldn't harm a flea."

"Well. Neither would Jake. But you wouldn't stand by while he did."

Alice doesn't answer for a moment. She's thinking that there are some things you can't tell anyone, no matter how close you are.

"It's not that simple."

Libby reaches out and puts her hand on Alice's arm. Alice stops rearranging all the items on her dresser top.

"Alice? What do you mean?"

"Nothing, Libby. I don't mean a thing. Except I can see how it might creep up on you sort of gradual. And maybe Herman . . . maybe it's like a sickness. And where would Grace go? She's got no folks to go home to. None of us do."

"Poor Grace. It's awful."

"I wish we could do something."

"But what?"

"Go visit her."

"What would we do with all the kids?"

"Where would we get the money?"

"Let's write and tell her to come home. She could at least come for a visit. It'd be easier for her to bring two kids here. I've never even seen her youngest."

"Herman won't let her come."

"I think a man like that should be locked up."

"Libby . . ."

"He shouldn't be allowed to have a wife. Or children."

Alice sits down by Libby on the bed. She looks down at her hands, folding and unfolding a lace-edged handkerchief in her lap. "Libby. When you stayed with Jake and me that time, while you were teaching, did Jake ever . . .? I mean, did he, well, did you ever think he was interested in you, that way?"

Libby nearly stops breathing. Alice can't think why she's asked Libby such a thing, except ever since Jake fell in love with that girl at Ordville, she's wondered. Libby is silent longer than she should be if there's nothing to say. Finally she blurts out, "My gosh, Alice. What's gotten into you?"

Alice is appalled to discover that tears are falling into her lap. She takes a deep breath and tries to laugh, the sound brittle and high. "It's this thing with Grace. I can't bear to think she's going through this all alone. And so far from home."

At dinner the kitchen is packed with rowdy children. Two glasses of spilt milk, one tipped into the bowl of green beans. Susan drops lime Jell-O in the lap of her yellow dress and cries. Jim and Frank kick each other until Alice separates them. Molly has to be told twice to stop singing at the table. Finally it's time for dessert, and Alice brings out the cherry pie. She's also made cupcakes with white frosting and dyed-green coconut. On top she's nested three jelly beans.

"If you kids want a cupcake, why don't you take it outside?"

The kids all grab their treat and scramble outdoors, except Stevie who rises and stands behind his mother and waits for her attention. Alice ignores him as long as she dares. Finally, she turns and he whispers in her ear. She nods her head.

Stevie turns to leave, and Alice rolls her eyes at Libby. "He's too grown-up to hang around these days," Alice says, and the women laugh. Stevie murmurs "bye" from the doorway, and Matt calls after him, "Don't do anything I wouldn't do."

"Let me try to put David down for a nap. Then I can enjoy my pie in peace." Libby picks up David who's so sleepy he's sliding out of the high chair.

The old truck starts up outside and Alice hears it backfire as Stevie pulls onto the road. The screen door bangs, and she steels herself for what she knows is coming.

"Mom! Mom!" Frank yells.

"Whoa, whoa, slow down," Alice says.

"You said I could go with Stevie."

"I never said for sure you could go."

"You did. You said we'd see."

"That's not yes."

"Damn it! You never let me do anything."

Alice rises from her chair and takes Frank by the arm. She pulls him over to the side of the room. "Frank. That's enough. Now, you have company."

"How come Stevie doesn't have—"

"I don't want to hear that. Stevie's a lot older."

"Sonofabitch!"

Alice leans down to whisper in Frank's ear. "Do I have to wash your mouth out with soap again?"

Alice watches her son clench and unclench his fists. His shoulders heave as he tries to wrench out of her grasp. She waits until he's calmed and then she tips up his chin and smiles at him. His eyes are blue and deep, the bluest of her three children's. "Go on, now."

Frank turns and shuffles out of the room. Alice watches him from the window. Soon as he's down off the steps, Jim asks him to play Work-up with the bat and ball. She's relieved when Frank grins. "Okay. But I pitch first."

By the time Alice sits at the table, Libby has returned from putting David down for his nap, poured all four cups of coffee, sliced the pie.

"How's that new job?" Matt asks Jake. Alice bites her lip and watches Jake to see how he'll react.

"Okay," Jake says. He stirs cream and sugar into his coffee. He sits there like a lump. Alice wishes he'd try harder to be friends with Matt.

"Alice got a letter from Grace," Libby says.

"Let's not talk about that," Alice says. "It's Easter."

"What's wrong?" Matt asks Libby.

"That no-good husband of hers," Libby says. "He hits her, and . . ." Libby glances up at Alice who shakes her head slightly. "I wish she'd leave him, that's all."

Alice glances at Jake, but he's looking down, working hard on his pie.

"We don't know the whole story," Alice says.

"I don't see how it takes much of a story," Matt says. "A man who beats on his wife is worthless."

"Anybody want more pie?" Alice asks.

"I think a man's got to protect his family. If he doesn't, who will?" Matt says this with complete confidence. Alice can't remember a time when she felt certain that she could protect her family. Who can, when you never know what's waiting around the corner? There's so much that can go wrong.

"Matt's starting our bomb shelter," Libby says.

"Won't that mess up your beautiful yard?"

Matt and Libby live in Sky Manor now, a new housing development in Sidney. Alice has seen Libby's grass yard, her low ceilings and picture window and thought she'd never be lucky enough to live in a home like that.

"Once it's done, I'll plant grass on top of it," Matt says. "It'll leave a hump, but that's not important."

Jake gets up and pours himself another cup of coffee from the percolator on the stove. "Anybody want more?" he offers. Only Libby holds out her cup. Jake fills it, his hand shaking slightly. He lingers a moment, standing by the window and looking out. He seems a million miles away to Alice, and she can't fathom what he's thinking. He's worse than Frank when it comes to knowing how to behave with company.

"Jake," she says, trying to bring him into the conversation. "Did you hear Matt's starting his bomb shelter?"

"I heard," Jake says. He comes back to the table and sits. "Like Noah, I guess."

Alice raises her eyebrows. This from a guy who attended church maybe four years in his whole life. He started going with her and the kids after that trip to Omaha, but ever since his spell, he refuses to go back. She thinks he's too embarrassed after the way he acted, following her in that old truck, parking outside the church and spying on her.

"Except God didn't tell me to do this," Matt says. "I don't believe in God."

"Oh, Matt. You do, too." Libby waves her hand like she's batting flies.

"I'm an atheist."

"He is not," Libby whispers to Alice.

"You mean, like the Communists?" Alice says, truly shocked. She's never heard Matt talk this way before.

"I'm no Communist. I just don't believe in God. If there is a god, he's incompetent."

"Don't, Matt."

"Wait, Libby," Alice says. "Why, Matt. How do you get through the day without God?"

"If there's a god, Alice, why's Grace stuck with a husband who beats her up? Why doesn't God do something about that?"

"I don't know why. We can't know why, but Matt, that doesn't mean God doesn't know. And care."

Matt laughs and tucks his arms across his chest. "I'll take my chances with my bomb shelter. See, I think we got to look out for ourselves."

They go on talking and arguing good-naturedly, although Alice is sincerely worried about Matt. She's thinking about his immortal soul and wondering if he'll end up in hell, and because she's focused on eternal matters, she doesn't notice when Jake slips away from the table and goes outside. She has no idea how long they've been sitting when Frank runs in, banging the screen door.

"Mom! Mom!" Frank yells. "What's wrong with Dad?"

Alice's hand flutters to her chest. Good god, has he died of a heart attack?

Matt grabs the flailing Frank and holds him still. "What is it, Frank? What's wrong?"

"Dad. He . . . he's locked himself in the car, and he won't open the doors."

"What?" Alice rises to her feet, tips her coffee cup over and scarcely notices the stain spilling across the table.

"That's crazy," Libby says and starts to laugh until Alice turns her white face toward her.

"Go on outside, Frank. I'll be there in a minute. Go on, now." Alice speaks mechanically. She scoots her chair into the table, takes pains to line it up just so. She looks at Libby and then Matt, an apology rising to her lips but unable to utter it. She turns and walks through the door, not looking back.

Their old Buick sits out by the shed, not a lick of shade around it. She can see Jake in the front seat, behind the driver's wheel, his head lying back on the seat cushion. All the kids are standing in the yard, several feet away but watching to see what will happen. She walks over to Jake's side of the car, chickens squawking and scrambling to get out of her way. The windows are rolled up, the lock buttons pushed down. Through the glass, she spots the keys hanging from the ignition.

She taps on the window. "Jake. Jake." He makes no move. For a moment she's terrified that he's dead in there, but she sees no blood, no weapon. "Jake, come out of there. You're scaring everybody."

He won't look at her.

"Roll the window down, then. Talk to me. What's going on?"

He doesn't move. He opens his eyes once, but shuts them again.

Alice stands a while and chews her bottom lip. Then, not knowing what else to do, she goes back to the house. On the way, she calls to the kids. "You kids, go on, now. Find something to do. Jake's just taking a little rest."

The kids peel off into various pursuits, Molly and Susan heading for the front steps off the living room to play Jacks, Jim and Greg pushing tractors around in the dirt. Frank stands planted, both hands shoved into his pockets.

Alice stops beside Frank. She drops her hand to his shoulder. Frank kicks his toe back and forth in the dirt.

"Frank . . ." she begins. She stops, not knowing what to say. She can't explain what she doesn't understand herself. Frank turns his face up to her, then knocks her hand free and races off toward the old corral. She watches him scurry over the garden fence and hunker down against the board wall. With her husband locked inside his car and her son hiding in the corral, Alice moves wearily back toward the house.

"What's going on?" Libby asks.

"I don't know. He won't talk to me." Alice shrugs and raises her hands.

"I'll talk to him," Matt says, and before Alice can protest, he's out the door.

"Is he like this often?" Libby asks Alice.

"No. Not like this," Alice says, but she hesitates.

"Oh, Alice," Libby says. She sits at the table and fiddles with her spoon.

"He's better. He's been seeing a chiropractor in Cheyenne."

"A chiropractor?"

"A pinched nerve or something. But he's a lot better. Like his old self. I don't know what happened today."

Matt comes in, then. "He wouldn't talk to me," Matt says. Alice is not surprised.

"C'mon," Alice says. "Let's get the dishes done."

Out of the corner of her eye, she catches Matt looking at Libby. Libby shakes her head slightly, and Matt takes the signal and goes off to the living room to find a magazine.

The two women pile up the dishes and get out two pans for wash and rinse. Alice heats water on the stovetop and pours it into the wash pan. Standing side by side, they move into familiar rhythms.

"I've always envied you," Libby says.

"Me? What for?"

Libby looks far away, drying a plate on one of Grandma's hand-embroidered tea towels. "Oh, you know. You got married first. Settled. You had a baby first."

"You have that new house."

"Yeah."

"And you get to stay home with your children. I wish I could."

"Do you?"

Alice stops washing for a moment and looks at Libby. Libby

says all in a rush, "I think your job sounds so fun, seeing all those women every day, having parties."

"Driving all over creation, you mean. Worrying about icy roads in winter. Going back to deliver, and they haven't collected their money. Hoping a tornado doesn't wipe out your home while you're gone. Or the kids burn down the house. I can make you a Stanley dealer if that's what you want. Our manager's always looking for new people."

"I could never do that. I'd be too nervous. But, oh, I don't know. Maybe I know how Jake feels."

Alice says nothing. What does it matter how Jake feels? People make do without having to feel good about it. What if she gave in and did what she felt like?

"Sometimes I lock myself in the bathroom," Libby says.

Alice rubs furiously at a soiled plate with a sponge. "Do you lock yourself up when you have company?"

Libby shrugs. "Not yet."

Something in Libby's voice stops Alice cold. She turns and looks at her, they lock eyes for a moment, and then they start to giggle. Alice forgets her hands are soapy and raises them to her eyes, wiping bubbles into her hair and that makes them laugh harder. She swipes a handful of suds at Libby and soon they're dipping their hands in the wash water and spraying water off their fingers.

"You two are as bad as little kids," Matt says. He's standing in the doorway. "You'll wake David," he warns.

"Oh," Alice says, straightening her back to stand at attention. She reaches into the pan of wash water, turns and hurls a handful in Matt's face.

"What the . . .?" Matt sputters, and Libby and Alice bang into each other laughing. They shriek and dance around the table when Matt gets his hands on the dish towel and snaps it at them, first one, then the other. He's aiming at Alice when Libby fills the drinking ladle with cold well water and dumps it over his head.

"Why you . . ." Matt grabs Libby by the collar and holds her while he dips water from the wash pan and flicks it into her face. Alice tugs at his arm, but he's planted like a fire plug. At the moment when she slips and falls to the floor, the baby starts to cry. The three of them stop suddenly, their clothes wet, faces dripping, the kitchen in ruin, Alice on the floor with legs akimbo, her skirt hauled up several inches above the knees. As if in slow motion they take in the damage, laughter frozen in their throats, and Alice, still sitting on the floor, can't stop her eyes from running, she's been laughing so hard and the water just keeps coming. "Oh dear, oh dear," Alice says, over and over, David crying louder in the background, and she leans forward to wipe her eyes with the hem of her skirt. "I'll get the baby," Libby says, tiptoeing from the room, as if she might break something. Matt reaches a hand to lift Alice to her feet. Standing in front of Matt, smoothing her dress down, running her hands through a tangled mass of hair, Alice turns away. "I'll get the mop," she says.

Not long after they finish with the dishes, Matt and Libby pack up their kids to head for home. In the drive, while they're saying their last good-byes, Matt gives Alice a hug and talks low into her ear.

"Alice," Matt asks. "Do you need anything?"

"Oh no, Matt. Don't be silly."

"I mean anything at all?"

"No, no. We're fine."

Libby squeezes Alice extra long, leans back and smiles into her face. She nods her head toward the car where Jake still sits. "Let me know," she says.

Alice smiles and waves them on their way. She turns and looks toward the raggedy Buick, but Jake's head is still thrown back against the cushion. Let him sit in his own stew, she thinks. She gathers Frank and Molly, tells them to come inside for a while. She's sewing in the chair, Frank working on his model car, Molly reading, when they hear the car start up. They listen while Jake drives out of the lane and down the road.

"Where's he going?" Molly asks.

"Who cares?" Frank says.

"Frank. I don't want to hear you talk that way about your father."

Frank pushes his model car away, scatters parts across the end table where he's working and heads for his bedroom. He slams the door, and Alice is left alone in the living room with Molly. She turns toward Molly, but Molly already has her head buried in her book, a collection of fairy tales their teacher found in the abandoned coal shed. All Molly does these days is read. Alice worries that she'll turn out to be as antisocial as her father, but right now, she's grateful for the quiet.

Stevie comes home around ten. He moves through the living room silently, careful not to wake Molly who sleeps on the couch. Alice hears the boys talking in their bedroom, figures Frank is filling Stevie in on Jake's odd behavior. Stevie comes to her door, pushes it open gently. "Mom?"

"Hi, Honey. Did you have a good time?"

"What's up with Dad?"

"He went for a drive."

"Do you want me to go and look for him?"

"No. He'll be back. It'll be all right."

Stevie stands in the doorway, unconvinced. She tries to smile at him. He's getting so grown-up. He looks like a scholar with his glasses and his brown hair cut in a flat top. He's driving into the high school this year. When he's not at school or some activity, he's down at Jerry's. She hardly sees him at all.

"G'night, Stevie," she says.

"G'night, Mom."

She lies awake in her bed, long after midnight. She thinks about Matt and how he says he doesn't believe in God. She couldn't get through the day if she thought there was nothing to this life, no promise. She couldn't bear it, and she's worried about Matt. She's worried about Grace, too, so far away and alone. She's worried about Frank, his brother growing up and leaving him behind. His father, the way he is. What will become of her boy, so tender he used to cover the autumn flowers to keep them from the frost?

For some reason, she remembers that time the deacons from the First Baptist Church brought a box of groceries. Two of them drove all the way out from town. They stood at her door with a box full of canned and dry goods, and she told them to take the food to somebody who needed it. Jake had stopped attending church by then, and not once had anyone bothered to call on them. Not once had anyone so much as asked about him. Let them keep their damn charity, she'd thought. But you can't blame God for what people will do. That's what she'll tell Matt the next time she sees him.

She hears the car pull in the drive. It must be well after 1:00 a.m. She hears the front screen door creak open, their bedroom door swing. She listens while Jake pulls off his overalls and hangs them on a nail at the foot of the bed. When he lies down beside her, she decides to stop pretending that she's asleep.

"Jake?" she says.

He doesn't answer.

"Jake. Where've you been?"

"Nowhere."

She waits a while to see if he will offer more. He doesn't.

"Jake, you have to learn to accept things."

Still no answer. She feels his body rigid in the silence. Is this the way it's going to be? she wants to ask. Is this what we have to look forward to?

He clears his throat, and she knows he's trying to say something. He starts a couple of times and finally gets it out. "That was a real nice cherry pie, Alice."

She lets go then and cries a little. Her emotions have rolled over her all day until she's thin as her pie crust. "Oh, Jake," she says, crying and hiccupping and half giggling until she feels safe again. She reaches her hand toward Jake, and he takes it in his, the way he always does. Finally she lies still, and her breathing slows and she lets herself sink. She whispers one last prayer, help us, help us, forgetting completely that the day she will waken to is Easter morning.

# SAVED

MOLLY, 1959

Molly's eyes are glued to the WANTED posters on the Elmyra Post Office wall. Ever since a year ago when Charles Starkweather slaughtered people across Nebraska and on into Wyoming, Molly's been obsessed with WANTED posters. She scans the faces memorizing clues, a mole on the cheek, a distinctive hairline, a dimpled chin. She focuses on the shifty-eyed man wanted for armed robbery. He's out there somewhere.

Alice stands by Box 476 talking to Mrs. Castano, a tiny Mexican woman who wears flesh-colored tape over one blind eye. Mrs. Castano smiles, nods and says Yes, yes, while Alice asks about her daughter and grandchildren. Molly has stood by while her mother raps on Mrs.

Castano's trailer door, bringing her End-a-Bug or Silent Maid or some other Stanley product.

"Molly, say hello to Mrs. Castano."

"Hello." Molly does not turn from the WANTEDS but flicks her hand sideways. When Charles Starkweather's picture was posted, he was only nineteen, and he had that girl Caril with him. He wore blue and white cowboy boots with a butterfly design on the toe, and Caril Fugate, fourteen years old, only three years older than Molly is now, wore bobby socks. They might have been anybody. They might have been the kids next door.

"You could have said hello." Alice says this on the way to the car, after she has dragged Molly away from the posters.

"I did."

Alice sighs, but doesn't bother to argue. When they get in the car, Molly pulls down the visor to check her reflection in the clipped-on mirror. She moves her lips around and tightens them until she matches her mother's expression. She snaps the visor up and watches the stores slide by on Main Street, picturing how the town must have looked to the ruthless desperadoes. She figures Charles and Caril had to drive straight through Elmyra. Depending on the time of day, she might have been crossing over to Bert's Drugs. She pictures herself strolling across Main, the strangers' car drifting by, her arm lifted in an idle wave while Caril and Charles decide whether to kill her or move on to their next victim. Or maybe she was standing outside the drugstore, checking the size and shape of her own legs against the crooked, knobby limbs of the polio poster child when Starkweather took her measure, sneered and declared her too scrawny to mess with.

Molly's mother drops her at the library. She never goes in with Molly because she's got too much to do to waste time reading.

"Don't forget you're helping with supper tonight. I'm tired after being on my feet all day."

Molly doesn't look back when the beat-up Buick pulls away from the curb. She's halfway up the stairs to the library before she remembers to turn and wave. Her mother has already pulled out of sight. Disappeared, Molly thinks. Abra-ca-dabra.

The heavy door groans. Inside, the narrow room smells of dust and leather. Miss Alsted's desk sits square inside the door in a pool of light drifting through a side window, yellow and soft.

Molly runs her hand over the spines of books, some so worn she can hardly read the titles. She chances on one with dog-eared pages. She takes the book down and lets it fall open and rubs her cheek across the printed words. Her eye trips over *cataclysm*. She has no idea what the word means but likes the sound of it. *Cataclysm*, *cataclysm*, a horse trots inside her head.

Charles Starkweather is not Molly's first introduction to crime. She knew a boy who burned down seven barns before he got caught. Everybody says Marvin Gates is a crook, even if he does have a law degree. Then, too, Banjo Morton had an affair with his best friend's wife, shot the husband while duck hunting and got off because the jury, twelve people who bumped into Banjo and his wife Elsie regularly at the Five 'n Dime, couldn't move beyond a reasonable doubt. Her own brothers once told Ronnie Techner they'd hang him if he didn't quit snooping around.

While Molly has *cataclysm* and thoughts of the criminal element trotting through her head, Miss Alsted walks around the corner. Molly slides the book back onto the shelf and turns toward the ancient librarian. Miss Alsted's hair coils in a tight bun with hairpins that stick out like miniature croquet hoops. Hose seams crawl up the backs of her legs, and she wears black, tied oxfords with heels. Molly stares at those shoes and thinks that she wouldn't mind being a librarian. Books all day. Quiet. Witch's shoes that fly you out the window. And whoever sticks up a library?

Miss Alsted hands her a book from off the wooden cart she's dragging behind her. It's from the adult section, thick with little print. "See what you think of this. You're not like a lot of the girls I get in here."

"I try."

"What's that?" Miss Alsted leans closer. Molly smells caked face powder and Evening in Paris cologne. The skin on Miss Alsted's neck hangs in droopy sacks.

"I try to be like other girls."

"Why?"

Molly grabs the book Miss Alsted is holding out to her. Yanking too hard, she bangs into a shelf. Books fall, one after another, the last one toppling long after Molly has slammed the library door.

On the way home, Molly slips in the side door of the First Baptist Church. After making sure Rev. Kane is not in his study, she sits down at the piano in the sanctuary. The knotty pine paneling glows from afternoon sun slanting through the yellow-and-pink paned windows. She opens the hymnal to "Showers of Blessing." She plays with arpeggios all over the keyboard and sings at the top of her lungs. She plays one hymn after every turn of a page, singing the words by heart.

When she's played herself out, she tiptoes to the center of the middle aisle and looks up at the empty cross. She stands there for a while, noticing how the gold curtains fall crooked behind the cross and over the baptistry. She turns around to make sure she's still alone, then drops to one knee and bows her head. Save my daddy, she says. She starts to rise and hesitates. God bless Mom, God bless Frank, and help Stevie get good grades so he can keep his scholarship and please make Linda Fritter like me, amen.

By the time she's ready to leave, it's getting dark and she knows she better hurry. She bumps into Rev. Kane on her way out the door. "Hey there, Molly. How's your mother?"

"She's fine."

"And your father? We don't see much of him."

"Gotta go." She shakes free of Rev. Kane's hand on her arm and runs up the street, her blue gabardine skirt flying.

For supper Molly peels potatoes, slices them, pours oil in a cast-iron skillet, turns the flame up high. Alice boils three eggs and opens a jar of home-canned beans. Don't peel the potatoes too thick, Alice warns. Okay. Watch out that the fat doesn't splatter all over. I'm trying.

Frank won't be home for supper. He's at football practice, and after that, who knows where? Maybe at the creamery on Main or smacking pool balls in the heady atmosphere of Carl's, where women and girls are not allowed. Ever since they moved to the edge of town, Frank's been making up for lost time.

When Jake comes in to wash up, the room goes quiet. He's been tinkering again and his hands are lined with grease.

"Where's the Boraxo?" He leans his head around the bathroom door frame. His wire-rimmed glasses sparkle in the light cast by the bare bulb hanging overhead.

"We're out. I haven't had time to go to the store. Don't use that towel," Alice says.

Jake stands with a towel in his hands. The pink one, worn and shiny. The one that always hangs opposite the sink.

"I got enough to do all day without having to wash up a towel every time you get grease on your hands. Use those paper towels."

*Cataclysm, cataclysm.* Molly beats a rhythm inside her head.

"We talked about politics today." Molly offers this at the table. She hands it to her father when she passes him the bowl of potatoes.

"Oh? You don't say."

"I like Ike. That's what the posters say. Do we like Ike?"

"He was a war hero." Alice rises and dumps more beans in the bowl. Bits of bacon poke out like tiny flags.

"I hear they're hiring again at the sugar beet factory." Alice sets the beans down with a thump.

"Is that so?" Jake lets this out with a sigh.

"Beulah Jacobsen said her son drove up there to Huntsville. They hired him right on."

"Next year, somebody else gets to be president." Molly kicks the chair with her heel. She kicks it harder and harder.

"Stop kicking that chair. For goodness sake. You're setting my nerves all on edge."

"Do you think it will be Nixon?"

"I don't know," Jake says. "Haven't thought about it."

"Beulah's son is only twenty-four. He's got no experience."

"Are we Republican or Democrat?"

"Jake?"

"Neither. Independent."

"Jake. What about that job?"

Molly's ears close up while her parents argue. She watches her father's hands shake. He's stooped low over his food. She knows he's been to doctors, some as far away as Cheyenne. Nothing wrong. What about these tremors? Can't say. What about this drooling? Don't know. Her mother looks so tired. *Cataclysm, cataclysm*, she drums inside her head. Alice is up from the table, slamming plates together, her mouth moving. Jake wanders from the table to the counter. Molly puts her hands over her ears and concentrates on Jesus. *Jesus saves, Jesus saves, Jesus, Jesus, Jesus saves.*

Later Molly finds her mother in the kitchen ironing. A bushel basket of sprinkled clothes sits on the table. Her mother's face is flushed from standing over the hot iron. She runs the searing tip up and down the stripes of Jake's work shirt.

"Mom?"

She doesn't stop working. She doesn't look up.

Molly bites her bottom lip. She wants to tell her mother about Linda Fritter's party and how she didn't get invited. She wants to say she slugged Tommy Gillespie because he said her dad was a bum.

"I've been practicing my penmanship."

"That's good. Maybe you'd like to write to Stevie."

"Yeah. Maybe." Stevie's never coming back to this one-horse town and nobody knows that but her. He told her. Don't tell. I won't. Be good. Okay. See you, Kid. See you.

At school Molly's one of the A students. She was doing math two years ahead out in the country school, so now she's coasting and waiting for her classmates to catch up. She's started playing in the band. Jake had an old silver saxophone, though some of the pads don't work. She sits beside Myron O'Banyon who has B.O. and scares her. He doesn't talk much, that's a good thing.

Some things she doesn't get right. Penmanship, for one. She practices push-pulls and ovals until her arm aches, but Mrs. Richter still gripes at her. On her report card, penmanship was a big fat C.

Some kids don't like her. They stop talking when she walks up to their jump-rope group. Phil Maylor called her Girf, and all the boys laughed and later she found out he meant it short for Giraffe. She studied her reflection in the mirror and started hiding her neck behind collars and turtlenecks. She developed a habit of holding her hand over her throat. She felt conspicuous. *Conspicuous.* A word that sounds like people spitting.

She's on her toes constantly, watching for signals. Linda Fritter is the girl everyone wants to sit by at lunch. Kids practically line up, waiting for Linda to choose. Linda says mean things, and kids laugh. Today Molly had been standing in line at the water fountain when Linda Fritter invited Barbara and Sandra to her birthday party. Linda looked straight at Molly and said in a too-loud voice, I can't invite everybody. Laugh, laugh. You wouldn't be able to afford a nice enough present. Joke, joke. Then laugh.

Molly hates Linda.

In books, people don't like other people all the time and nothing falls down. In a book, she could tell her mom about Linda Fritter's party, and Alice wouldn't say, For goodness sake, what did you do to her? In a book, she could throw Linda's coat down a well. Joke, joke. Then laugh.

Molly's father is reading in the living room. After telling her ironing mother good night, Molly stops behind his chair. Lamplight glows off his shiny head. A white crocheted doily is scrunched behind him, *National Geographic* spread across his lap. Molly catches sight of pandas.

"Dad?"

Jake turns his head to find her. He looks for her, and she steps to the side of the chair. Jake's hand trembles, his sleeve catching on the doily over the chair arm. She places her hand over it. "Good thing I'm not graded on penmanship," Jake chuckles. Molly loves it when he laughs.

"Nancy Fritter didn't invite me to her party."

"Oh?" Jake leans his head back to look in Molly's face. Behind his glasses his eyes are rheumy, and his jaw swings out of control. She wants to pet him, like she does her cat Winston when he gets his foot caught in the door.

"I don't care." Molly shrugs and leans over for a good-night kiss. Jake's whiskers prickle against Molly's lips, and he smells of aftershave.

Nancy Drew. The Hardy Boys. A book of fairy tales her country school teacher rescued from the coal shed. A white Bible with a zipper. These are the books Molly owns. She's read all but the Bible cover to cover. The Bible she knows in snatches. *Vengeance is mine, saith the Lord. Keep watch and be sober* —. There's a plaque above her bed that says *Jesus saves*. She stares at it every night to find out the secret. Why doesn't Jesus save everybody?

Molly's room is only a converted closet, but it's the first time she's had a room of her own. She sleeps on a cot Stevie pilfered from an abandoned river cabin. She has the little desk Jake made for her and her Grandma's old dresser, and there's even a window with curtains her mother sewed from a faded bedspread. Molly piles her stuffed animals one on top of the other, a yellow dog and a purple bunny. She rolls them together in a soft blanket and tucks them into the crook of her arm. She booby-traps her doorway with a chair. If the shifty-eyed burglar comes, she'll be ready for him.

Her dad has rigged a pull chain so she can reach it from her cot when she's tired from reading. She opens the book Miss Alsted gave her. *Jane Eyre*. Chapter 1. Jane is banished from the drawing-room intended for contented, happy, little children. Jane finds a bookcase. Jane hides in the window seat with a book in her lap.

Molly and her mother sit in a cloud of dust under a circus tent. They sit in the front row on rickety bleachers, rough with layers of peeling paint. Lights glare from strings of bulbs threaded across the big top. It's Saturday night, two days after Linda Fritter's birthday party, and Jake has stayed home.

"Here come the dancing dogs." Alice squeezes Molly's arm, and they laugh at the poodles dressed in starchy skirts.

Two clowns show up. They wear polka-dotted overalls shaped like a barrel, big shoes, red wigs, fake noses. One trips over his own feet and sprawls face down in the dirt. The other pulls petals off a daisy. His mouth droops at the corners, a big sad face with red mouth painted down, and people laugh.

White horses spill into the ring, manes braided, tails high. Trapeze artists hang by their knees, arch high on wide swings and drop and flip. Somebody gets shot out of a cannon. Laugh and laugh.

Then the elephants enter as a parade, three of them, two huge ones and a baby, bedecked with sparkly headbands and embroidered blankets. Wrinkly grey skin, absurd trunks, ears big as dinner plates, legs the size of the columns on the First Baptist Church.

A man and a woman sashay with whips crackling. The man barks orders like staccato bass notes. He wears black trousers and a black cut-away coat. The woman oozes from a scanty pink swimsuit, arms and legs bluey-white, her hair in tight yellow curls.

The elephants hold hands with their trunks and tails, stack themselves up in a pyramid, tip up on their front legs, rear back on their hind legs. The crowd cheers and whistles. Molly and Alice clap their hands.

A drum rolls. A voice from a loudspeaker booms, "Now for the most dangerous trick of all. All eyes on Big Baby on the south side of the ring."

The crowd hushes. The man leads the biggest elephant over in front of Molly. He reaches behind Big Baby and draws the doll woman out by the arm. He pinches her arm so hard that white marks spread under his fingers. The woman's eyes turn glassy and round. She shakes her head from side to side. The man speaks into her ear, and they both look up at the crowd, smile, and wave. The man pushes the woman by the arm, pressing her flat on the ground. She clamps her lips together. Molly tugs on Alice's sleeve.

"Sh-h-h. Hush now."

The man walks Big Baby over to the woman. The drummer plays another roll. The man taps Big Baby behind the knee with his baton and Big Baby lifts one front leg. Big Baby swivels her massive, crushing foot over the woman's face, inches above her pert nose and rouge-dotted cheeks. Molly sees tears slide from the corners of the woman's eyes and pool in her ears.

"Mom." Molly tries again. The crowd has risen to its feet, pulled like taffy. The man in the black coat coaches the elephant to swing its foot to the ground. The woman has risen to her feet, trembling and smiling. The man's hand clenches her upper arm. *Jesus, Jesus. Jesus saves.* Molly chants this like a mantra, but no one pays attention. The crowd erupts into cheers and applause.

Molly stands in the front row chewing on the paper cone left over from her cotton candy. The crowd hoots and laughs, and she starts to cry. The woman, standing not three feet away from her, catches her eye and winks. Joke, joke. Then laugh.

Did you have a good time? Sure. What'd you think of the elephants? I dunno. Some act, huh? Guess so.

Molly goes straight to her room after the circus, no good-night kisses, no stories of clowns and dancing poodles. Her mom and dad are arguing, but she doesn't listen. She doesn't care.

*Cataclysm.* She looks it up. *Violent upheaval or disaster.* She stares at herself in the mirror. Stretching her neck until the cords pop out, she sticks her tongue out at herself and puts her hand up to touch her fingertips to the girl's in the mirror. She makes a fist and flexes her bicep in preparation for the shifty-eyed thief who's still on the lam. She rolls her dog and bunny into their blanket and stands looking at the *Jesus saves* plaque over her bed. Be careful, she says to herself, not at all sure what she means.

# I WONDER WHY-WHY-WHY-WHY

FRANK, 1961

Frank's been working in the hayfields for three summers before the October when his Grandma Preston dies. Finally. She's seemed ancient to him as long as he can remember. Skinny and stooped, a hump on her back, bib apron over a dark patterned dress, navy blue or black with white squiggles. Big buttons. She carried a black pocketbook tucked under one arm, her false teeth loose and clattering. White hair snugged back in a strangled bun, hairpins and a net.

He knots his tie sitting on the edge of his bed and looking in the mirror above his dresser. He hates this cramped, squatty house. His room holds this dresser, the four-poster bed that once belonged to Grandma, and the deep freeze. Everything's crammed so tight that he has to scramble over his mattress to get to the closet. Anybody opening the freezer has to kneel on the bed and heft the heavy lid.

They moved here while he was away at hay camp. He came home, filthy and bone weary after wrestling calves and bunking with fourteen other snotty-nosed, underpaid boys, and this is where they brought him. Little hole of a house down by the river. They've only lived in town for a couple of years. The first place got sold out from under them, and his mother couldn't find another rental house in town. There's only a garden between this house and the landlady's, old Mrs. Tweed. She's a true bitch, nagging his mother constantly about the rent, even when it's not overdue. He's pretty sure she poisoned their dog, although Buster was miserable living in town and had gotten mean. Still.

He's not very good at knotting the tie. He takes it out to start again when Stevie steps into the doorway. His know-it-all college brother. Just because he won a scholarship to the university down at Lincoln, he thinks he's smarter than Einstein. He came home, that first autumn they lived in this house, stood in the living room with the crowded furniture, cocked his head toward the bedroom where Molly slept on a cot and his parents in a double bed, then toward the back porch where there was a more-or-less bathroom with a shower stall and said, Mom, you can do better than this. What does he know about it? He left for college the day he graduated from high school. He's never set foot here since except for an occasional visit when Alice treats him like the prodigal son, goes hog-wild, makes them clean the house from top to bottom, cooks steak and mincemeat pie.

It's true this place is a pit. When he'd walked in here, home from the hay camp, he couldn't believe it. Not quite as bad as the beet shack, but they were kids then. His dad sat in the living room, reading. Frank walked into the kitchen, turned on all the burners on the stove, turned them off. He could barely open the

refrigerator without bumping into the table. He was banging cup-
boards open and closed when his mom came in. She threw her
arms around him, leaned back to look in his face. He said what
was on his mind: If I ever get married and have kids and don't
have a job, I hope somebody takes out a gun and shoots me.

"Want me to do that for you?" Stevie's looking sideways into
the mirror. He's standing in the doorway, tapping his college-boy
toe and watching Frank mangle his tie.

"I got it."

"It's time . . ."

"Jesus. I know it's time."


He and Stevie drive together to the funeral. Molly's singing, so
she's gone ahead. Alice and Jake went early to view the flowers.

"Want to drag Main?" Stevie's got a shit-faced grin on his face.

"I thought we had to be on time."

"We got a few minutes."

Stevie heads his blue and white Fairlane down Main Street.
A perfumed skunk swings from the rearview mirror, tiny red
jewel eyes. Frank leans over and turns on Stevie's radio, flips
through the channels. The Shirelles are singing "Will You Love
Me Tomorrow." He sits back to float on the music when Stevie
reaches out and turns down the volume.

"Matt and Libby'll be here, I suppose."

Frank nods his head.

"Mom says Matt's been transferred to California?" Stevie's chat-
ty, all of a sudden. Frank's wary, but he answers.

"Yeah. Mom's pretty broken up about it."

"Did Billy make it home?"

Frank shrugs. "Yeah. I guess. I think he's staying down at
Mary's. They'll be up today, too."

"Be pretty tough on Mary now."

"Yeah," Frank agrees. He wishes he could light up a cigarette, but he guesses he better not. College boy might tell on him.

"You hadn't been down to Sidney in a while, had you?" Frank asks this, knows the answer. He wants to rub Stevie's face in it.

Stevie shakes his head.

"Well, it wasn't no picnic, in that house. Some kind of government housing."

"Oh yeah, I remember all that. Picket fences. Tiny."

"Were you there after Grandma came back from Florida and moved in with Mary?"

"Christ, Frank. I haven't been gone that long. Of course. Lots of times."

"Well, then. You know."

Stevie maneuvers the car around the island at the end of Main, starts back down the opposite way. They pass the Trail Theater, Brenner's jewelry store, the Five 'n Dime, Bert's Drugs, the Gambles Store before he opens his mouth again.

"She still got that paint-by-number Last Supper?"

Frank grins. "Right over the couch."

They chuckle together.

"Mary probably won't be able to afford to stay there without Grandma."

"Yeah." "Runaway" comes on the radio, and Frank concentrates on the beat.

"Are Ruth or Helen home? Or Nick? He still living in Denver?"

"Yeah. Nick's in Denver. He ain't coming. Helen and her husband, what's his name?"

"Joe?"

"Yeah, Joe. They live in Phoenix, I think. Who knows where Ruth is? Last I heard, Las Vegas."

Now they're passing the county courthouse, Elmyra Equipment, the creamery.

"Molly's singing?"

"Yeah. Mom's idea."

"She any good?"

"I don't know. People say she is."

The Masonic temple, Ebson's Chevrolet, Safeway. They'll be out of street pretty soon, and Frank's sure Stevie hasn't gotten around to the topic yet. Stevie turns left at the Conoco and heads west.

"Where you going?" Frank looks at his watch.

"Little spin around the pits."

"What time's this thing start anyway? I got 1:15."

"Two. It starts at two."

"What the hell? You told me 1:30. What's all the rush about?"

Stevie doesn't answer. He turns onto the drive to the sand pits, past the house of the blind man who sells brooms on Main, past the trailer park. When they get to the lakes, Stevie goes around both the big ones in a figure eight. He drives slow. "Goodbye Cruel World" floods the car, and Frank would laugh but he knows Stevie wouldn't get it. On the second time around, Stevie clears his throat.

"Dad been working?"

So. Finally, Frank thinks.

"Hell, no."

"What about the sugar beet factory?"

Frank shakes his head. His dad tried that graveyard shift. Couldn't sleep during the day.

"You know what happened with that," Frank says.

Stevie looks at him and then back to the road. When Stevie was home last year for Thanksgiving, there'd been some terrible scenes. Jake accused Alice of sending Stevie to the factory to spy on him. Said he'd seen him there, watching.

"Something's wrong with Dad," Stevie says.

Frank laughs out loud. No shit, he wants to say.

"You don't remember him, the way he was. I saw him shoot a pheasant once, on the fly, 125 yards with a shotgun. He built machinery out of nothing but a pile of screws and bolts and an idea in his head. He overhauled this old Ford of mine, took the engine out and completely redid it."

"Hell, he shot a deer last year. He and mom dressed it out on the kitchen floor."

They're on their third loop of the lakes. Frank wonders why Stevie doesn't just stop. Maybe he can't. Maybe none of them can. After a while Stevie tries again. "He just can't handle the pressure of a job."

Frank kicks his foot against the floor. He wants out of this car. He can hardly breathe, even with the window rolled down. "Can we get this funeral over with?" he says.

Billy's standing out in front of the church when they pull up. Frank's heard about Billy all his life, but only seen him one or two times. He's tall and lean, like a cowboy without the chaps, sandy-haired and glasses. He sticks his hand out to both of them. Stevie grabs first, and they shake.

"Well boys, you're a sight for sore eyes."

He speaks with a thick southern accent. Frank has to laugh, because the story on Billy is that he hates Florida, has from the day he set foot down there, but he married a Florida girl, someone Grandma didn't like, which may have been the appeal, and now he's stuck there. Got a kid or two, but they're home with their mother.

They murmur a bit, voices hushed the way people do at a funeral. Frank wonders what Billy thinks of his dad or if he's seen him yet. They write letters all the time, and Frank can tell from the few he's read that Billy practically worships Jake.

They file into the church, and from the back Frank sees his mom lift her head, turn around and spot them. She motions them up to the front with the family. He walks, kind of dazed, behind Stevie who's taking up all the shine since he's the college boy. Libby and Matt are there, but none of their kids. He guesses they have better things to do on a Saturday. Mary's on the center aisle next to Jake, and Billy slides in beside her. Stevie decides to cross around in front of the whole section of pews rather than crowd in front of Mary. She's so wide they'd never get by. Stevie takes his place next to Alice, and Frank next to Stevie.

Frank doesn't listen to what the minister has to say. Molly gets up and sings in a wobbly alto. Not too bad, but he wouldn't want to do it. Sing in front of all these people. He sees Molly turn white afterward and wonders if she'll make it through the rest of the service without bawling. She's like that, nervous and touchy.

His shoes hurt and his tie's killing him. He reaches up to loosen the knot a little. Reverend Kane's moving in for the big finish now, and soon the organ starts to swell. The ushers take the rest of the church folks out first. There's quite a few here, which is a surprise since nobody knew Grandma, but he guesses they've come for Alice's sake. Not his dad. Most of them don't give a hoot if his dad lives or dies. Why should they, but aren't they supposed to be Christians?

His girlfriend's house is across the street from the Baptist church, and while walking down the aisle behind his mom and dad, he wonders if Beth will be watching from an upstairs window. He thinks about standing up straight, how maybe he'll put his hand over his left side a little, not his heart exactly, but to kind of suggest that he's hurting. Girls like that simpy stuff.

He's caught off-guard when the row of mourners stops. He looks ahead and sees they've opened his grandmother's casket at the back of the church where they all have to go past. He fights to keep his breath steady; a few red spots dart in front of his eyes. He's only a few feet away, beside Stevie and behind Alice and Jake, when Mary stops and bends over the coffin, her white, wavy-haired head bobbing low. She kisses Grandma's leathery cheek, and Frank feels something rise in his gullet. When his dad stops to gaze, Frank keeps his eyes straight ahead and grabs the pew on his right. He holds on while he feels himself sway. It's hot in here, and he has to steel himself not to bolt out the door.

He will not look, and as soon as he gets past the coffin, down the vestibule steps and to fresh air, he walks to Stevie's car. He sits in the open door with his head hanging between his knees until he can breathe again. He's forgotten all about Beth and whether or not she's watching. He struggles to keep his break-fast down.

"You all right?" Stevie asks when he opens the driver's door to get in.

Frank sits upright, testing, testing, yeah, he's okay.

"Let's go," Frank says.

"The hearse goes first."

They sit silently while Mr. Layton, the mortician, maneuvers the gray hearse around the corner. Their parents follow, with Molly, Matt, and Libby in the car. Billy follows with Mary. Then it's their turn.

They take the same road leading west that they took to the sand pits except they keep on driving past the Assembly of God church, past the bait store, another couple of miles and enter the Oregon Trail Cemetery. They wind around a bit and stop where Gramp's and Carlene's graves are laid.

"How old was Billy when his mother died?" Frank asks this to be saying something. He doesn't give a rat's ass.

"I don't know. Young."

They get out of their cars in silence. The grass has turned

brown, a few yellow leaves still clinging to the trees. They huddle around the two old stones and the fresh grave, and while the minister reads, Frank lifts his gaze north toward the river. He can make out the rows of trees, follow the line of it all the way toward town. He thinks about Billy losing his mother like that. That would be tough on a kid. He looks at Alice standing with her arm through Jake's. She looks like she could be Jake's daughter, but he's old for his age. He studies Jake, watches how his hand trembles, sees his jaw fall away slack. Maybe he does have something bad wrong with him. He can see how they could've gotten used to it, little by little. Alice is wearing a blue dress, a short fall coat over it. She complains all the time about how fat she's gotten, but Frank thinks she's pretty. She's wearing a hat shaped like an upside-down beehive, white feathery stuff on it, high-heeled shoes. She's tough, his mother, and before he knows it, he's got tears in his eyes because he's thinking about Billy losing his mom like that.

Billy comes up to them while they're walking toward their cars. He wants filled in on Stevie's big plans. Frank hears words float by, engineering, space, Sputnik, he doesn't pay much attention. His brother's a brain; let him win the Cold War single-handed. He's got the words to "Runaway" flying inside his head. Run away. That simple.

They stop by the car, and Billy's tone gets more serious. "It's sure too bad about your dad," Billy says, his voice soft and liquid, concern deep in the hollows of his face. Before they can answer, Alice has grabbed Billy by the arm.

"You'll come back to the house, won't you?"

Billy's face opens when he sees Alice. Frank watches the change and knows more than anyone has bothered to tell him.

"Why, sure Alice. Mary and I'll stop around a little while."

"Boys?" Alice raises her eyebrows at them. They both nod,

murmur something unintelligible, and as soon as they get in the car, Stevie turns to him. "Wanna shoot some pool?"

By the time they're back from Carl's everybody's gone, which is perfect. That house couldn't hold more people anyway. Alice is fit to be tied, of course, lecturing them about family and responsibility and Billy only home one day out of ten years, or maybe twenty years, Alice doesn't worry about details when she's sermonizing. They hang their heads in mock sorrow, and they get through the afternoon until about five o'clock when something starts it.

Later Frank can't remember exactly what got said. Something about the four-poster bed, that's all he knows. He hates the stupid thing, and secretly he feels creepy about sleeping in his dead grandma's bed. Stevie thinks it's a treasure, something to pass down. One of them shoves the other. Then they're out on the lawn pushing each other around. Frank's not smaller anymore, the way he used to be, and he looks at Stevie and laughs, infuriating him the way he always did. Stevie tears into him a little harder. No fists, they're just wrestling, but there's an edge to it, and soon neither of them can back off. Molly's standing on the porch, Stop it, Stop it, hopping from one nervous foot to another. They keep on hauling away at each other like two bull elk. There's a moment when Frank sees the old Stevie, his buddy and foe, when Stevie squares off against him and automatically moves to lift his shirt collar and bite it. It's over in a flash, he drops the collar instead of putting it in his mouth, but Frank remembers how he did that all the time, sat on top of him, punched him in the arm, his face flaring with anger and chewing on the collar of his shirt. He got into such a habit that once in a while, in the summer when they'd go without shirts, Stevie actually bit his own shoulder. The thought of those days raises the fire in Frank, and he dives toward Stevie and topples him to the ground. There's heat in it now, and he fights for his life. Legs and arms scrambled, Molly yelling Stop it, Stop it like a background rock-and-roll beat, they keep at it until Frank is bone tired and his limbs drag, but he won't stop. The sun slides down, sinks, the light wanes, and still they roll over each other, punish each other. Finally, after an eternity of mindless battle, their dad steps out on the porch. "Here now, you boys, stop that." He says it in the mildest possible voice, and relieved for an excuse, they pull apart, snot running down their faces, drool, their shirts soaked with sweat and stained from dirt and grass. Frank moves toward the house without looking at any of them, his bones ache, his shoulders burn, he's tired beyond all belief and triumphant.

That evening while Stevie's away in his Ford looking up some old buddies and before he gets back to share the bed, Frank goes out to the shed. He unlocks the padlock and rummages around amongst his dad's tools until he finds a saw with the right heft. He wants it to feel good in his hand. He walks back in, past his mom who's lying on the couch with the paper, past his dad who's dozing in the chair, past Molly who's writing in her stupid diary. He closes the door to his bedroom and strips off his shirt. He opens his window and lifts out the screen. His dad has lost his mother today, that's what he allows himself to think. That withered-up woman who sent him a birthday card every year with a one-dollar bill tucked inside, her chicken-scratch handwriting, Love Grandma. He lets himself remember that his dad was once a boy, and he's thinking of Billy and his mother dying young when he saws the posts off the bed and pitches them, one by one, out the window.

# LITTLE DEATHS & MINOR RESURRECTIONS

ALICE, 1974

A mild day in August and Alice is drinking a cup of black coffee, looking out her kitchen window and thinking that today might be the day that Nixon resigns from office. She voted for him twice, three times if you count 1960, when he lost to Kennedy. She had believed in his innocence even when her college-educated children, who all live far away from here, laughed at her. She takes it personally that Nixon lied.

She's left Nixon behind and is running through a mental list of her busy day when she hears Jake stir at the table behind her. It will take him half the morning to finish his coffee and toast and get his pills down, the ones she's counted out for him. His Parkinson's symptoms are worsening, but he's at his maximum tolerance for medication. When he gets too much, his thinking goes astray. Last week she came home and found all four burners of the gas stove flaring. Alice can't imagine what they'll do when she can't leave Jake alone to go to work. She tries not to think about it.

"Jake. Art Bellingham's going to stop by and take a look at the hot water heater."

"This morning?" Jake lifts hazel eyes to her. He's oddly not wrinkled. His face is thin and haggard, but still handsome. Dr. Morgan at the University Hospital in Omaha said he had the heart and lungs of a fifty-year-old. He's lived clean all his life, but something in his nerves sneaked up on him, and now this.

"Art'll be gone by noon. I'll be finished with Mrs. Benton's party by then."

"The courthouse closes up at four."

"I wish you'd get that idea out of your head."

"You said you'd take me."

"I know I did. I think it's a foolish idea, that's all."

"They close up at four."

Alice rinses her cup under the sink and sets it in the strainer. She opens a kitchen cupboard with a mirror inside, tidies her short, bottle-brown hair, tubes lipstick onto her mouth. She adjusts the belt of her green jersey dress and wishes she could lose fifteen pounds. She used to be thin before she started this job and had to eat rich desserts every day so as not to offend her hostesses.

"Tell Art to check that pilot light on the furnace, too."

After years of renting, they own this house, and Alice is not about to let it go to rack and ruin. She found the house herself, signed the papers against Jake's wishes. One house or another, it didn't matter to him, but he hated living in town. She can't leave him alone out in the country, and he ought to know that.

Jake fingers the paper cup with his pills in it. "Where'd you put my pills?"

"I put them away. I told you. I'll be back at noon for your next dose."

He doesn't like it that he's not in charge of his own medication. She's taken it over lately because she worries that he'll accidentally overdose himself. She can't have him burning down the house.

She leans over to kiss his cheek. Their eyeglasses chink together, and she pats him on the shoulder.

As she leaves the house he calls after her. "The courthouse closes up at four."

She's late getting back from Mrs. Benton's party. She had to drive twenty-six miles out in the country, east and then north up into the Sandhills, and after selling $126 worth of Stanley Home Products to nine women, Mrs. Benton wanted to stand and talk about her married daughter who's getting a divorce. Alice listened, of course, because she loves her hostesses and because she's smart enough to know that this is why they keep booking parties instead of driving into town for their supplies.

Alice drives back to town in a rush, bumping over dirt ruts, flying over hills. She knows every quirk of these Nebraska roads. Twenty years ago when she first started this business, farm women were isolated and grateful for a chance to gather and have a little fun. Then, too, it was the fifties and more women stayed at home in the small towns. All the other Stanley dealers have called it quits, but Alice still ekes out a living, except she's often late getting home and Jake worries.

She checks her watch every five minutes. She's an hour and a half late for Jake's next dose of L-Dopa. She parks in the drive and runs in the back door and up the half flight of stairs to the kitchen. God almighty, Jake's standing at the counter, his eyes wild. Wobbly on his feet, jaw sliding right and left, a butter knife clenched in one fist. On the kitchen counter he's piled white bread slathered with margarine and maple syrup. She glances at the table and sees two more stacks thrown together like a madman's block tower. He's stuck in a repetitive pattern and can't get out. The way the doctor described Jake's illness makes her think of a merry-go-round when you feel sick and want off but can't get your foot on the ground.

She gently places her hand on his arm. "Jake, why don't you sit down now?"

"I thought I better make some lunch." He sits, and she pries his stiff fingers off the handle of the knife.

"You made enough sandwiches for an army." She sweeps soggy bread into the trash.

"I know." Jake's hand rubs the top of his head. "Better get my pills."

She leaves the kitchen and heads for the spare bedroom, for the shoebox she's tucked high in the closet behind an old overcoat. On her way past the bathroom, she notices that all the drawers are pulled out of the vanity, the medicine chest wide open. He's been looking, then. He spilled a bottle of aspirin, and some of them crunch under her feet out in the hallway. Vaguely she wonders what aspirin does to carpet, but she doesn't stop. The important thing now is to get his next dose down him. Sometimes when he gets like this, his swallowing mechanism freezes up and then they have a hell of a time.

She gets the pills and grinds them with a mortar and pestle. She finds a jar of apricot baby food in the refrigerator and mixes in the fine pink powder. She has it in front of him within ten minutes of entering the house, but she is sick with guilt.

When he's quieted a little she tells him. "After this, I'll leave a day's supply at a time. I'll buy one of those plastic tray things at Bert's and lay them all out. You won't have to wait if I'm late."

"Okay," he says. His voice rattles, his throat clogged with phlegm.

After they've had a cheese sandwich and a glass of milk and his hands have stopped trembling, she asks him if Art made it by to check the hot water heater.

"He said it looked okay to him. I told him to check that valve, so he replaced it."

Alice smiles. She pictures Jake hovering over Art and inspecting his work. Jake's hands might be shaky, but he hasn't lost his know-how for machines.

"He sure was interested in that old Victrola," Jake offers, as Alice rises to start the dishes.

"Had he ever seen one?" Art's maybe in his thirties, too young. These days, half the world is too young.

"Said he's seen one or two, but they didn't have the cylinders. He wanted to hear it working."

"So you got it down?"

"Art took it off the shelf. I showed him how to wind it up and put the cylinder in."

"Which one did you play?"

Jake grins at her shyly. "Guess."

She shoots him a coy look. "You played 'Redbird.'"

He's standing by her now. Her hands are covered with suds and she puts one on either side of his face and tilts up to kiss him full on the lips.

"He forgot to put it back on the shelf. I put the box of cylinders away."

She leans against him as he loops his arms around her. "That's okay. I'll get it later," she says.

"Courthouse closes up at four."

She laughs and pulls away to finish up. "I know. Why don't you go rest a bit. Turn on the television and see what Nixon is up to."

"I don't care what he's up to."

"I do. It's history. Turn it on. I can hear it from here."

She watches him trudge across the dining room carpet on the way to their bedroom. "And this time take your shirt off," she calls. She hears him laugh and wave a hand at her. It's a joke between them ever since she came home one day and found that he'd cut the buttons off a new shirt that Molly had sent for his birthday. He wanted to lie down and couldn't unbutton it. Not wanting to wrinkle it, he'd cut all the buttons off. After that, Alice sewed Velcro on all his shirts.

While Jake is resting, Alice sits for a few minutes in a chair with her feet up. She's watching Nixon backpedal and haggle and reading the *Elmyra Newsblade* at the same time. What a world, she's thinking, when the president of your country lies.

They park on Main Street in front of the courthouse, a two-storied tan brick building with four majestic columns. Black letters spell out the name of Meredith County and the founding date, 1909. It takes Jake a while to walk up the entry flight of stairs. Their voices echo in the cavernous space.

They find the license examiner's room and there's one bad moment when the officer, a young man who's not from Elmyra but comes in for the day from another county, mistakes Jake for Alice's father.

"Bring your father in here," the officer says, as if Jake has to be led by the hand.

"My husband," she says. Jake walks in by himself and sits down in a chair. The wood floors creak and smell of polish and large windows glare with August sun.

"Well, then," the man grins at Jake, "looks like you got yourself a young filly."

She bristles, but Jake says nothing. He's focused on the job he has to do, and he has never cared much for what people think. She is thirteen years younger than Jake, but his illness makes him look older than he is, and none of this is the examiner's business. She doesn't like this young man's attitude and has a good mind to set him straight. She's hesitating in the doorway when Jake turns around.

"Go on, now," he says and waves her away.

There's still plenty of light when they leave the courthouse. Jake's elated because the examiner renewed his driver's license. He hasn't sat behind the wheel of a car for years. The examiner made him drive, while Alice watched out the second-story window. Jake maneuvered their green Pontiac around the courthouse block and parked it out front without so much as a jerk or stall. Alice believes most people, including Jake, can do anything if they set their mind to it, and that's why she suggests they drive out west of town where they used to live and let Jake take a turn at the wheel.

"I don't know." Jake is waffling, and they're not even outside the city limits. "I thought I ought to have my license in case of an emergency. If you went to the hospital, I'd want to visit you. But driving around on those gravel roads. I don't know."

They cross the bridge over the North Platte River into North Bridge, which is nothing but a ghost town these days. Another mile and they reach the turnoff to that old beet shack where they used to live. The ditch teems with goldenrod, and along the creek that runs through here, she spots a wild pink rose. The fields of sugar beets and beans look good this year. Alice drives a few more miles, across the railroad tracks, and then she stops in the middle of a flat stretch of road.

"C'mon. Get over here." She steps out of the car and goes around to his side. He can't scoot and lift his feet over the center hump, so she coaxes him out of the car and around to the driver's side. All the way he grumbles and grouses and she pretends not to hear him, telling him how beautiful the day is and lucky it's not that hot for August and he's going to feel so good taking them for a spin the way he used to when they were courting. She gets him settled and then she puts herself in the rider's seat, slightly toward the center in case he needs help, but not so close to crowd him.

He takes off with a jump, but soon he smoothes out. He's doing it. He's driving, and he grins and starts to relax. They go out past Degraw School, nothing now but an empty lot since the school burned down. He angles the car left past that beet shack where they lived and on out to the Wentworth place. She figures his head is full of memories, as hers is, but they don't talk about it, not the good times, nor the bad, they just sit in the car and ride and he's behind the wheel and it feels good.

"Want to go out to the dump?" he asks.

She laughs. Down a little draw, there used to be three trees, cottonwoods lying in the low marshes, and the third tree was a country dump. People unloaded their old cots and refrigerators and used magazines there. More than once they'd found something useful. "I doubt it's still there," she says.

The road dead-ends near the river, and they stop and listen to outdoor sounds for a while. Insects buzz and meadowlarks sing and the wind rustles the leaves of the cottonwoods. Here, the prairie grass sways and bends. Cotton-winged milkweed seeds float and stick to their windshield. They hope to see a deer, but it's too hot this time of day. Finally, they manage to get the car turned and headed in the opposite direction.

It doesn't happen until they come over that little rise just past the Osborn farm. Jake's getting along fine, his foot steady on the accelerator and he's moving slow, maybe twenty-five miles an hour. They come up over that rise, and there's a tractor pulling a harrow coming toward them. The harrow takes up most of the road, so they'll have to move out on the shoulder a bit.

"You'll have to get over," Alice reminds Jake.

Jake keeps moving steadily ahead. Alarmed now, Alice says again, "Jake, move over. He can't go anywhere with that thing."

Jake yanks the wheel and, at the same time, his foot presses harder on the accelerator, and the car swings wildly from one side of the road to the other. The tractor looms closer. Alice makes a frantic grab for the wheel, screams at Jake to lift his foot, and just as the tractor and harrow barrel down on them, she manages to wrestle the car out of Jake's control and they land safely, but in the ditch.

Neither of them speaks, their breath having escaped them. Alice sees that Jake's face is white and his hands tremble. She needs air and rolls down the window, smells the goldenrod crowning amidst the ragweed, wonders how she can notice that at a time like this.

"What the hell do we do now?" he finally asks.

Alice notices in the side mirror that the tractor driver has not stopped. Probably some kid, she thinks.

"We'll drive out." Alice keeps her voice calm and steady.

"You do it."

They try opening the car doors but they're wedged by the sides of the ditch.

"You'll have to," she says. "Just start it and put it in gear."

He won't look at her, his head turned out the window, but he makes no move to start the car.

"C'mon," she says gently. "We can't sit here all day."

"Somebody'll come along."

"C'mon. We're getting out of here."

She overrides him, the way she has to much of the time. She starts the car and pushes him over against the door so she can get both hands on the wheel. She stretches her leg so her foot reaches the accelerator. The first time she guns the engine too hard and the wheels do nothing but spin.

"I told you we better wait." Jake's bony shoulder gouges her arm. She can feel the outline of his hip.

She tries once more, and this time they move forward. She turns the wheel to climb up out of the ditch and except for the tiny moment when the car teeters and threatens to roll on its side, it's no problem.

"We're all right now." Without another word Jake heaves his door open and moves around to the rider's side. Alice slides behind the wheel and they move off. They don't speak, it's forgotten between them, but she knows he will never drive again. You can't get ready for this, she thinks, while she grips her hands tightly on the wheel and drives slowly to town.

After they've gotten settled through supper, Alice goes to the basement to do a load of wash. She decides to put the old Victrola back on the shelf. She turns on all the lights, but she can't locate the Victrola anywhere. It's funny, because the wooden box with the cylinder records is sitting on the shelf right beside the vacant spot.

"Jake," she yells. "Jake."

She keeps looking during the time it takes Jake to cross the living room and come down the stairs. She's relieved to find "Redbird" in the box, along with "Painted Lady" and "Hawaiian Sunset" and all the others.

"Where'd you say you and Art were looking at that old Victrola?"

"Right there on that bench." Jake points, but there's nothing there.

"Look at this, Jake. All the records are here. Why would somebody take the Victrola and not the records?"

"I don't know, unless they didn't know we had the records."

"But nobody knew we had the Victrola except Art. He's the only one."

"You aren't thinking Art Bellingham walked off with it, are you? Why would he do anything that obvious?"

"Who else could it be?"

"The door's wide open. The UPS guy delivers your Stanley stuff straight into the basement. He could've seen it any time."

"Jake, UPS didn't come today. Nobody's been here but Art. I'm calling the sheriff." She starts up the stairs.

"Hold on, now. There's no reason to disturb Gus at home, is there? Let's just wait 'til morning."

"I'm calling him right now."

It doesn't take long for Alice to tell the sheriff the story, and it takes only about fifteen more minutes before the sheriff calls back to report that he's talked to Art who says he doesn't know a thing about their Victrola. The sheriff asks her if they keep their doors locked, when he knows no one locks their doors in this town. Then he tells her there's not much to go on and not much he can do.

"I told you to wait 'til morning," Jake says when she reports to him.

"What difference would it have made? Art would've just had longer to get his story straight." She flounces down on the couch and pulls her feet up under her. Jake's reading in his reclining chair and he doesn't set his paper down. She thinks about turning on the TV, but it's across the room. She picks up a book and without opening it puts it back down.

"I'll never hear "Redbird" again."

"Now, Alice. When was the last time you listened to it?"

He knows she hasn't had that Victrola out for years. They moved it from one house to another packed away in a box. She doubts Molly even knows they had it.

"That's not the point. I always knew I could. Besides, it was your parents', and that means something."

Jake waits a while, then says, "You don't think it was Art, do you?"

Alice studies for a moment. "I don't see who else, but no, I don't think Art would do that."

"Well, then, let's just leave it at that."

Later Jake goes to bed ahead of Alice because she likes to listen to the ten o'clock news. When she slides in beside him, she reaches over and takes hold of his hand. She can tell by his breathing that he's not asleep.

"Maybe tomorrow, they're saying. He's going to be impeached."

Jake grunts.

"What about that Gerald Ford? Do you think he'll make a decent president?"

"They're all about the same," Jake says.

They lie in the dark for a while. Not able to stop herself, she reviews the losses of the day, the little deaths that creep up on you when you're not looking. The Victrola. Jake's driving. Nixon. She turns her mind, a right angle, and thinks about how tickled Mrs. Benton was with her party premiums, the glow of goldenrod lighting up the ditch, the quiet of sitting by the river. She thinks of her loved ones and prays, as she does every night, for their safety and happiness. When she feels that she's almost ready to drift off, she lets loose of Jake's hand. He reaches out to touch her on the breast. She lies absolutely still and wondering. He hasn't touched her this way in years. His hand travels to her soft stomach and he moves, gentle and soothing the way he always did. After a few circular motions, he pats her and says, "That will have to do you." And it does.

# LOVE SONGS

## MOLLY, 1979

H er brothers kneel on the roof inspecting shingles while Molly helps her mother trim the overgrown spirea by the front porch. Alice gathers unruly swatches in her arms, and Molly wields the hinged cutters. The blades are rusty and dull, a sure sign that her dad has been dead for a year.

"He left notes all over the place," Alice says. She's wearing tan, knee-length shorts, a brown T-shirt out over the waistband. On her feet, ankle socks and tennis shoes. She's lost weight. Her hair is still curly, dyed dark, though she insists she's not that gray.

"What notes?" Molly stops to wipe sweat off her forehead. She wears contacts, and the kicked-up dust irritates her eyes. She's a head taller than her mother, thin like her dad. She's got his hazel eyes, too. She's wearing shorts and an orange tank top, sandals. On her left arm, beads of blood form along a scratch from the bristly shrubs.

On her knees now, Alice trims the grass away from the bricks lining the rose bed. "Cardboard tags. Things like how to clean the oil in the car. How to light the pilot light on the furnace."

Steve and Frank *bang-bang* on the roof, getting things done. They're scientists, both of them, Steve an engineer, Frank a chemist. Steve probably designs missiles and spy satellites, though he'd never tell Molly, even if his job wasn't classified. He lives in Southern California, plastic world. Wife, two kids. Frank works for the railroad, deals with chemical spills. He lives in Omaha. Wife, three kids. Molly lives in Minneapolis. Husband, two kids. She's an art photographer.

She envies her brothers' lucky genes. They got their fathers' mechanical aptitude plus their mother's practicality. She, on the other hand, inherited her dad's artistic sensibility, a dubious trait clouded by his history. She's sure her mother worries about what will become of her. She wonders herself. Another thing, she's the only Democrat.

She follows her mother to the garden plot behind the stucco house. Her mother yanks at weeds, and Molly bends with her to the task, her nose down among the Big Boy tomatoes and the stinky marigolds that are supposed to discourage aphids. She thinks about those cardboard tags her dad left lying around. She pictures his shaky handwriting, the grade-school loop of the letters.

"I guess he thought he was taking care of you at the end," she says.

Alice grunts, stops bending, and squats on her heels. "He always took care of me."

"I thought you took care of everything."

"Then you didn't notice. He did things."

"Like what?"

Alice sits back, brushes hair out of her face. "Set the alarm clock every night."

From the house they hear the phone ringing.

"I better get that," Alice says. The screen door bangs behind her.

Molly rests her hands on her hips, looks up at the roof. Her brothers are on their feet, surveying their work. She wishes she had her camera. She'd catch them in the lens, looking manly and distant, silhouetted against a bright sky, higher than the world on which she stands.

Later they gather around the dining-room table, Molly, her brothers, and her mother. They're awkward together without the insulation of spouses and grandchildren, even though the three siblings worked hard to arrange this visit. They wanted to help their mother sort and throw, make a few repairs on the house without the pandemonium that goes with seven children. Frank's wife, Letty, and his kids are staying fifteen miles south on her parents' farm. Frank drives out there to sleep at night. Steve's wife, Willa, and his son and daughter are visiting Willa's parents on their farm up by Valentine. Steve's family flew into Denver, rented a car, dropped him off on their way. Paul's got Molly's daughters at his parents' house in Plattsmouth. She flew from Minneapolis to Scottsbluff, which cost a bundle. On Friday the spouses and all the kids will gather for the weekend, the anniversary of Jake's death, though they won't talk about that. Not in front of the grandchildren.

"What's left?" Frank says.

"Are you done with the roof?" Alice asks, dishing up chocolate cake.

Frank looks at Steve. They nod. Molly scrapes the thick frosting off her cake, leaves it in a sugar heap on the side of her plate.

"There's the garage," Alice says. She sags down in a chair. She looks tired, dark circles under her eyes. She's on blood-pressure medication. "All your dad's tools."

"Why don't you just leave them here?" Frank says.

Frank's elbow rests on the table. He waves away the chocolate cake. He's put on a few pounds, though he's still the best-looking of the bunch. Blond curls. Blue eyes like Alice's.

"Anything you boys can use, I want you to take."

"Just let them be. We need tools when we're out here," Frank says. His voice rings with mock patience, overly loud.

"Leave what you think you need. And take what's left over." Alice's voice rises, too. Petulant and sing-songy.

"I got all the tools I need," Frank says.

"I thought you might want something of your dad's."

"Steve's flying. He doesn't have room for tools. Just leave them be."

"No, I want them cleared out. I can't use them."

Frank laughs, low. Shakes his head. "All's I'm saying is, we don't want to have to go buy a wrench if we're out here and you need your toilet fixed. Why not just let them stay out there? They're not in your way."

"Somebody could get some use out of them. If you don't want them, then I'll give them to the church."

"That's crazy," Frank says.

"We'll look at them tomorrow," Steve says.

That ends the sparring match. Molly breathes a little easier. It's lost on her why Frank and her mother enjoy this battleground. His tactics work, she has to admit. He's the favorite one.

Alice stands and stacks their CorningWare plates, white with tiny green flowers on the rim. Molly picks up bowls of leftover ham and green beans, carries them to the kitchen. She runs hot water in the sink, squeezes in Stanley dish soap. Frank's made it as far as the front door. Alice trails behind him, saying good-night. She reminds him to drive carefully. Molly throws a glance into the dining room, sees Steve sitting with his head on his hand, propped on the table. He'll be out to dry dishes soon. He's the thoughtful one.

While Alice takes a bath, Molly and Steve read in the living room. Neither of them sits in their father's recliner. She's in Gramp's old oak rocker, beside the pole lamp with tiny stuffed bears clamped up the shaft. Around the base of the lamp, seven sleeping ceramic dwarfs crowd the floor, a hand-made gift from one of Alice's Stanley hostesses. Steve sits in one of two blue velveteen swivel rockers, his feet propped on a matching ottoman. She's flipping the pages of a novel, Toni Morrison; he's reading a Robert Ludlum spy thriller.

"How do you think she's doing?" Molly asks. She keeps her voice low.

"Good." He shrugs.

"She doesn't sleep."

"It takes time."

She considers his responses. This is how he copes, by keeping a distance. He didn't come home for her wedding.

"Frank still won't talk to me," she says.

Steve shifts in his chair. Like a stranger on an airplane, he's signaling that he doesn't want to talk.

"He leaves the room when I walk in," she says.

Steve looks at her.

"Metaphorically, I mean."

"He's a guy of few words," Steve says.

Molly sighs. Turns a page in her book. "He never understood what I was mad about in the first place."

Steve won't ask her. She knows this. He won't give her any reason to go on with this explanation. She wants to. She wants to tell him every detail of the fight she had with Frank over what their mother should do with the impressive (on her income!) amount of money she has saved. Frank insisted that a broker friend of his advise her. Molly wanted her mother to manage her own affairs. After all, that's what she's been doing all her life. What's different about now? She got furious because he wouldn't listen to her, kept butting in, using that tone he gets like he's overriding a tantrum-throwing toddler. She stomped off in a rage, cried, and walked around five city blocks, and when she straightened up and came back to the house, aware that it was hard for her to admit her mother might need help, Frank met her at the door to his home with a signed affidavit: I won't have anything to do with Mom's finances. She tried to tell him what had set her off, but he wouldn't listen to that either. Now he avoids her.

"I was scared," she says. She's the one who talks of feelings.

Steve puts his book down and grins at her, a cock-eyed slanted slash on his face. He looks boyish and a little goofy, her favorite of all his expressions. "When you were little you weren't afraid of anybody."

"Really?" She can't focus on this version of her younger self.

"You'd go up and talk to perfect strangers."

Molly looks at her shy, older brother. The one who wouldn't go to the bank window to cash a check in this small town where their mother's lived all her life.

"That's funny," she says. "I felt scared all the time. Even now. Sometimes I lie awake waiting for something bad to happen. Like a habit that's hard to break."

"Most things turn out okay," he says.

She stares at him. Wonders if he really believes that.

"What about dad's life?" she says.

Shrugs again. "Everybody has problems. Dad was just a hippie before his time."

She nods, amazed at his capacity to find a label that pacifies him into sleep at night.

"I asked Frank that question," she says.

"What'd he say?"

"He said Dad was a stubborn sonofabitch when he was living, and he was a stubborn sonofabitch the day he died."

The next day Steve and Frank make piles of tools in the garage. Molly and her mother go through Jake's clothes. He didn't have much, a few shirts and pants.

"Would Paul wear these?"

"No, Mom."

"Would Frank or Steve?"

"I doubt it."

They fold the clothes and press them into boxes. The gesture does them in, like laying the man in a tomb. They both grow quiet and tight-lipped.

When the phone rings Alice springs to it, relieved to hear a voice from the outside world. It's her friend Verna, and Molly knows she'll be a while. Molly opens the top drawer of her father's bureau and takes out a stack of small notebooks held together by a rubber band. She sits on the edge of the bed and flips through the pages. He recorded bits of history: prices of bread, the date of the Apollo moon launch, the flight of migrating sandhill cranes. She comes across a few sentences titled Unbelievable Shots by Jake. There, her father describes shooting a pheasant on the fly, stepping off the distance afterward at 125 yards.

In one notebook, dated 1965, she finds the address of a nerve specialist in Cheyenne. A list of symptoms—pain in arms and legs, back ache, tingling—a question wondering whether these might be related to an old injury from a car accident. Not long after that, Jake was diagnosed with Parkinson's Disease.

Molly closes the memo pads, stacks them in her father's drawer along with a couple unused handkerchiefs, a billfold, a few ties. She picks up his pocket watch and holds it in her hand, the weight of it nestling in her palm. He used to carry Juicy Fruit gum for her in his pocket. A coin purse with a silver snap clasp. He carried a coin purse and this watch and a pocket knife to remove slivers and gum that only she liked.

"That was Verna," Alice says, coming back into the bedroom. She lifts the watch from Molly's palm. "I thought Steve or Frank would like this. The other one can have Gramp's."

"Oh," Molly says. She feels punched, the air gone out of her. She never met Gramp, but she sees her dad with that watch tucked into a small pocket in his bib overalls.

"His wrist watch is there, if you want," Alice says. It's a Timex, cheap. A convenience he agreed to in these last years. It's not him.

"Could I have some of these ties?" Molly asks.

"He has newer ones in the closet."

"I like these." A loden green with a yellow emblem down the middle, another silver and blue striped, all of them 1940s vintage except for the tourist tie with Mount Rushmore on it.

They finish up, knot string around the boxes. They keep the pocket knives and tie clasps for the grandchildren. The unused things—boxes of handkerchiefs, gloves, a wool muffler, all gifts for the man who needed nothing—Alice sets aside to give to the church. Molly takes the neckties into the middle bedroom, lays them in the bottom of her suitcase and rests her hand on top of them. She sighs with a long shudder, then closes the lid.

That afternoon Molly and Alice are summoned to the garage to see the boys' work. Frank stands outside the lifted garage door, near the alley, smoking. Steve points out the categories: keep, give to neighbors, throw away. Each of her brothers has claimed a small pile: a handsaw, a metal file. They've laid one or two things aside for Paul, if he wants them. Molly nods her head. Alice crouches by the throw-away pile. She lifts a hammerhead, a flat piece of steel, unable to part with what was once his, or maybe it's that Depression-era mentality. Molly moves toward the open door to stand by Frank. She hears Steve say, "You want us to do this or not?" Alice chuckles. She can take this from Steve, the one she trusts.

"Looks like you've done a day's work," Molly says to Frank. His white T-shirt is sweat-ringed and grimy. He's wearing jeans, sucking on his Marlboro.

Frank grunts, his eyes turned west. He doesn't look at her.

She waits him out. She's good at silence when she has to be. She turns her eyes west with him, looks out over the neighbor's garage and trees to where the sky is starting to hemorrhage.

"Think I'll take off early today," Frank says.

"Letty and the kids okay?"

"Yeah. They're fine."

"Mom and I cleaned out Dad's closet and drawers."

He nods.

"Did you find some tools to keep?" she asks.

He throws his cigarette butt on the ground, grinds it with the toe of his boot. "Most of that stuff's so old, it's not worth much."

Later, after Frank is gone, when they've all declared that they're tuckered out and going to bed, Alice says of Frank, "I know today was hard for him. He's so sentimental."

The next day Molly and Alice are downtown getting milk at the Jack 'n Jill, picking up a prescription at Bert's Drugs, stopping in at the post office where Molly still remembers the box code—3A

to the right, 2H to the left, 1E to the right—when they run into
Wilbur Fenway. He's a slight man, thin and wiry, dark wavy hair.
Molly remembers his wife, Maxine, a sickly woman. A son—Ron,
isn't it?—who was behind her in school. He holds the door for
them, says, "Afternoon, Alice."

"Well, hello Will," Alice says. She backs up, makes a porch
of her hand to shield her eyes from the sun. Will drops the door
closed and steps over beside her.

"This Molly?" he says. Molly shakes his offered hand, a firm
grip. "You're all growed up," he says.

He grins at Alice. Alice looks up at him, blushes. Surprised,
Molly stammers, "Uh, Mom, I'll wait for you in the car."

She sits in the driver's seat and tries not to stare while Alice
and Will carry on a short conversation. Alice bobs her head a few
times, laughs. Once Will cradles Alice's elbow.

When Alice gets in the car, she starts fingering through the
mail. "My goodness," she says. She sounds breathless. "I hardly
ever get anything worth reading anymore."

Molly starts the car, herds it around the island at the top of
Main Street. "I always thought Will was a nice man," she says.

Alice waves her hand. Doesn't look at Molly. "His wife died
last year."

"Oh?"

"She'd been sick a long time."

"Like Dad," Molly says.

"Way worse than Dad. She had a brain tumor at the end, but
she was mentally sick for years."

"Sounds like you know quite a bit about it."

"Oh, everybody knows that." Alice's voice sounds tinny and
light.

She waits until they are nearly home, in the alley and pulling
in the garage. Then she says, "Have you been seeing him?"

Alice laughs. "Don't be silly. You know how many single women are in this town? I counted them up one day—142—and those are just the people I know."

"So?"

"So a lot of them are younger than me."

Alice wends her way to the house while Molly lingers in the car. She thinks of the glow on Will's face. Her mother is fifty-nine years old, a young grandmother. She hasn't had an easy time of it. She's still working, selling Stanley, and now part-time at the hospital on the janitor staff. It's not likely, of course. Alice is right about that. Consider the odds. But then, you never know. Molly yanks the rearview mirror around, studies her face, wipes her cheeks. She shakes her head and wonders what has become of her, that she is undone by the kindness of strangers and this hint of possibility.

That afternoon after Steve and Frank have trimmed the bushes, chopped down the dead locust tree, and before Frank heads out to the farm, they take a drive out to the cemetery. The four of them stand over the graves, Gramp and Grandma Preston, Carlene, and now their dad. Alice wants them to see the double stone, her name already on it, everything but the final date.

"There's room for me and one more," she says.

They stand silently, not knowing what to say. They decide to stroll through the small cemetery, and Alice recites tales about the people she has known. In the old section under a towering cottonwood tree, Molly stoops and picks up a waxen leaf. She folds it in half, holds the bottom and the two edges taut and blows into it. She rolls her fingers to change the tone, makes a sound like a wolf whistle.

"C'mon," Frank says. "You can do better than that."

He stoops then, picks up a leaf, folds it identical to hers, blows.

He plays a few notes, badly out of tune, but recognizable as the opening line of "The Star Spangled Banner."

"Listen to this," she says, and toots out *Row, row, row your boat.* They are all laughing by now, she and Frank throwing down crimped leaves and picking up new ones, battling each other to see if Alice and Steve can name that tune. Finally they put their heads side by side and play *Amazing grace, how sweet the sound.*

"Where'd you learn to do that?" Steve asks.

"Can't you?" Frank says.

"No," Steve says. "I never saw anyone do that before."

"Dad showed me," Molly says.

"Well, sure. Dad used to do it all the time," Frank says.

Molly looks into Frank's eyes, the eyes like her mother's, past the surface blue and deep into what they know between them, what nobody else on this earth knows, what it was like to be a child in that house during the bad years after Steve was gone. Don't ever leave me, Molly wants to say. But instead, she blows on cottonwood leaves until her lips are numb.

That night after Frank has left for the farm, they drag out the old phonograph and the records Jake cut. There's his voice, melodic and low, saying year after year on New Year's Eve, "well, it's been a purty good ol' year." Alice's voice is girlish, giggling, "I don't know what to say." Molly's brothers sing *My home's in Montana, I wear a bandanna, my spurs are of silver, my pony is gray* . . . They sing so earnestly and sweetly that it knots her throat. They sing Bible school songs, *the B-I-B-L-E, yes, that's the book for me.* She was young during these years, there's not much of her voice recorded except for one badly out of tune version of "Away in a Manger."

"I thought you were the musical one," Steve says.

"What are you laughing at?" Alice says. She's tone deaf, so the joke's lost on her.

"That's the way Mom taught it to me," Molly says. She feels guilty, this comment at her mother's expense, but Steve laughs.

They find the record of Jake singing the songs he wrote. They fall silent, listening while his unaccompanied voice sails in from the past. He sings about Nebraska sunsets and hills and prairie grasses. Last is the love song that he wrote for Alice, "Sweetheart, Say You'll Be Mine."

Steve lifts the needle off the record when it's finished. "Didn't Dad publish that song?" he asks.

Alice clears her throat to speak. "He thought he was going to be a big success. He paid somebody. Nothing ever came of it."

"You mean a vanity press?" Molly says.

Alice shrugs. "Is that what you call it?"

"I thought he couldn't read music," Molly says.

"No, he sang, and somebody else wrote it down."

"What happened to it?" Steve asks. He's replacing all the records in the brown paper sleeves, marked and dated in their father's hand.

"Oh, they sent us about twenty-five copies. They're around here somewhere."

After they've all gone to bed, Molly gets up and roots around in the closet of the spare bedroom. This is the closet where the vacuum cleaner is stored, the off-season clothes, the ironing board. On the top shelf she finds a cardboard box, lifts it down. Inside are copies of sheet music, mint green, with a purple silhouette of a man and woman kissing against a nighttime sky. She sits for a long time holding the open copy of her father's song, *I love you my dear, and I always want you near,* her fingers playing on her lap as she reads the lines of music. She feels her father standing behind her, the way he used to do when she played the piano. She sits very still and listens. After a while, she opens her suitcase, places one copy on the bottom along with the 1940s ties. She replaces the box in the closet. She should tell them where these copies are, but she won't. She can't say why.

The next day all the spouses and grandchildren arrive, the house filled with laughter and chaos, whining and banging screen doors. The children range from Steve's ten-year-old son to Molly's youngest daughter who is two. When Paul drives in, exhausted after a tedious ride with both kids in car seats, he waits his turn while the girls scramble into Molly's arms and she swings them around the front yard. He crosses to her, his gait uneven from the bad hip that kept him out of Vietnam. He kisses her, then says, "I thought none of us would survive that trip." When the commotion has settled and the others' attention is off him, he says quietly to Molly, "You okay?"

"Yeah," she says, surprised to discover that she means it. There's a lot to tell him, but for now, she squeezes his hand.

Surrounded by these children, Alice thrums with energy. Molly is swept up along with everyone else in the day's activities: a picnic in the park, swimming at the sand pits, games of Hearts for the older ones, puzzles and stories for the younger ones.

Much later when the kids are all asleep, bedded down on the floor or in the basement or on the porch, when the spouses are drinking coffee and telling stories in the kitchen with Alice, the three of them wander outside, Steve, Frank, and Molly. They stand under the night sky shot with stars and blazoned by the Milky Way. Molly looks at the upturned faces of her brothers, and for that brief moment, the old loneliness falls away. She knows them as no one else does. She can see all the way down to their good intentions. If the three of them have become largely incomprehensible to each other, still they are bound, as families are, by blood and history. In this moment she's glad that she has her father's heart, aching and full of yearning to keep those she loves near. Tomorrow she may be gripped by the terror of the dark, she may look down long corridors and quake, but tonight, fixed on the star-lit faces of her brothers, she is unafraid. She knows they will not speak of love or any other thing. Instead they will hover in silence, until one or the other will say, "Well, good night then," and they will peel away.

In the Flyover Fiction series

# UNIVERSITY OF NEBRASKA PRESS

*Also of Interest in the Flyover Fiction series:*

## Jackalope Dreams
By Mary Clearman Blew

Played out against the mythology of the Old West—a powerful amalgam of ranching history, Marlboro Men, and train robbery reenactments—the story of the newly orphaned, spinsterish Corey is a sometimes comical, sometimes poignant tale of coming-of-age a little late. As she tries to recapture an old dream of becoming a painter—of preserving some modicum of true art amid the virtual reality of modern Montana—Corey finds herself figuring in other dramas as well.

ISBN: 978-0-8032-1588-7 (cloth)

## The Floor of the Sky
By Pamela Carter Joern

In the Nebraska Sandhills, nothing is more sacred than the bond of family and land— and nothing is more capable of causing deep wounds. In Pamela Carter Joern's riveting novel, Toby Jenkins, an aging widow, is on the verge of losing her family's ranch when her granddaughter Lila—a city girl, sixteen and pregnant—shows up for the summer.

ISBN: 978-0-8032-7631-4 (paper)

## Because a Fire Was in My Head
By Lynn Stegner

From her childhood, in which she was held captive to a mother gone mad, through her adult life, which unfolds as a mesmerizing sequence of men, abandoned children, and perpetual movement, Kate Riley's story is one of desperation and remarkable invention, a strangely American tale, brilliantly narrated by one of our most original writers.

ISBN: 978-0-8032-1139-1 (cloth)

---

Order online at www.nebraskapress.unl.edu or call 1-800-755-1105. Mention the code "BOFOX" to receive a 20% discount.